THE
SNOW
HAWK

THE SNOW HAWK

LESLIE MᶜFARLANE

Methuen Publications
TORONTO LONDON
SYDNEY WELLINGTON

Cover design by Alan Daniel

ISBN 0 458 91700 1

Printed and bound in Canada

1 2 3 4 5   0 9 8 7 6

Contents

THE
SNOW
HAWK

Chapter 1:
The Renegade of Bitter River

The jagged peaks and pinnacles of Crazy Mountain loomed bleak against the northern sky. At the base of a sheer wall of rock stood a tiny cabin, almost buried in drifts that came within a few inches of the roof. The snow had been cleared away to reveal one frosted window that stared out over the wilderness like a cold and watchful eye.

At this window stood the Snow Hawk.

This cabin, far off the beaten track and miles from the traveled trails of the Bitter River country, was his refuge. He was a hunted man, an outlaw with many crimes marked against his name. The cabin at the foot of Crazy Mountain was an ideal hiding place. The steep cliffs prevented attack from the rear, and the position of the cabin gave him a clear view of many miles of wasteland sloping toward the mountain.

One of his huskies had uttered a warning howl. It had sent him leaping toward the window. There he crouched, peering out over the hard-packed desert of snow. Off in the distance a tiny black speck moved against the white background. The Snow Hawk's eyes narrowed and he reached for his binoculars.

The powerful glasses revealed that the black speck was a man, a sled, and four dogs. But the man's face was a blur, and at that distance the Snow Hawk could not identify him. He put the binoculars aside and turned away from the window. He took down his rifle, tested the action, slipped a few shells into the magazine.

For the Snow Hawk, being an outlaw, had enemies.

It was hard to believe that this tall, bronzed young giant was one of the most notorious adventurers in the

Northland, a man whose name was feared by many and blessed by few, an outlaw whose spectacular exploits were whispered in all the lodges of the Bitter River. He was a straight, clean-cut young man with an air of reckless good humor. His mouth was not hard, but it was determined. His eyes were not cold, but they were clear and alert. He looked like a man who sought adventure as the spice of life and who welcomed danger with a smile.

The huskies in their shelter at the back of the cabin were howling in a mournful chorus. The Snow Hawk went back to the window and again watched the approaching team.

The Snow Hawk had little fear of the police, although it was said in the Bitter River country that Corporal Maxwell of the Mounted had sworn to capture him dead or alive. His most dangerous enemies were among the lawless criminals who sought to exploit the Indians and the white trappers. The Snow Hawk was an outlaw who warred upon outlaws.

The dog team sped swiftly over the hard-packed snow, drawing steadily closer to the cabin in the lee of the mountain. The Snow Hawk picked up the binoculars again. Was the newcomer friend or enemy?

This time the face of the man on the sled leaped into clearer view. The Snow Hawk smiled, with a nod of satisfaction. "Mandziak!"

Although the Snow Hawk was a hunted man, he had many friends in the wastelands. The trapper named Mandziak was one of them, their friendship dating from the time the Snow Hawk had routed a pair of fur thieves who had made off with a three months' catch of pelts from Mandziak's cabin. He was one of the few who knew that the tiny cabin at the foot of Crazy Mountain was the refuge of the Snow Hawk.

Ten minutes later, as Mandziak drove up, the Snow Hawk unbarred the door and stepped outside.

"Hello, Mandziak! What brings you here?"

The trapper, a swarthy, thickset man who looked like an amiable bear in his dark parka, got up from his sled as the dogs flung themselves panting in the snow.

"Trouble," he said briefly.

The Snow Hawk's eyes narrowed. He knew that Mandziak had traveled far that morning and that the journey was important.

"Trouble for me?"

Mandiziak nodded. "Better move out of here."

"Why?" asked the Snow Hawk calmly.

"Corporal Maxwell is on the trail again."

The Snow Hawk whistled softly. No less than three murders were chalked up against his name. And Corporal Maxwell was one of the ace man hunters of the Mounted. "Come inside," he said.

"I got this straight," explained Mandziak when they were in the cabin. "A trapper came north along the river this morning and he told me. He got it from someone at Stone Lake. When I heard the news, I figured I'd better tip you off."

The Snow Hawk was quite calm. Mandziak admired the young outlaw's nerve. In the Bitter River country, men did not take Corporal Maxwell's name lightly.

"Where is Maxwell now?"

"He's on MacLean's place on Lonely Lake. He's after you," said Mandziak with a worried frown. "That's the one reason he's up here. 'I want the Snow Hawk!' he said. That's what he told the man. And you know Maxwell's record."

"Yes," smiled the Snow Hawk, "I know."

"You'll have a good start if you clear out of here right away."

"Maybe I'd better stay where I am."

Mandziak shook his head. "He'll find you here if you do. Everybody knows you haven't been on the river in the past few weeks. He'll figure you're out here in the back country." Mandziak had a healthy respect for the ability of Corporal Maxwell.

"You're right," said the Snow Hawk at last. "I'd better hit the trail."

He went over to the stove, made tea for his visitor. They did not discuss Corporal Maxwell again. Mandziak was a law-abiding man and it went against the grain to oppose them, but the law of friendship came first. He owed a great deal to the Snow Hawk, and he knew too that this husky young man was no ordinary outlaw. There were many things about the Snow Hawk that he did not understand.

"Is it true, what they say about you?" he asked curiously. "Did you really kill Whisky Ben Keever?"

"Was he a friend of yours?"

"No friend of mine," declared Mandziak.

"I didn't kill him."

"And that fellow they found in the mountains back of Blizzard Bluff?"

The Snow Hawk shrugged. "Bedell? I guess some would say I killed him although it was an accident. I'm not denying it. If it hadn't happened the way it did—well, you wouldn't be talking to me now. I'd be lying dead somewhere in a snowbank."

"I can't figure you," said the trapper, shaking his head. "You act like a square guy. And those fellows were outlaws. But just the same—"

"Just the same, they're dead. Forget it, Mandziak. I've stolen furs. Who did I steal them from? Fur thieves. And I gave the furs back to the men who lost them. I held up Baldy Kirk, the gambler, and took every cent from him; but what did I do with the money? Gave it back to the men he cold-decked. I've been blamed for killing that Mounty on the Thunder Mountain trail, but that's wrong. I've been blamed for half a dozen crimes I know nothing about. As for the men that died, I was on the short end every time."

"You'll have a fine time proving it if Corporal Maxwell catches up with you," muttered Mandziak.

The Snow Hawk grinned. He tapped Mandziak on the shoulder. "Corporal Maxwell is not going to catch up with me," he said.

In spite of Mandziak's warning, the Snow Hawk was in no hurry to leave his cabin. It was several hours after the kindly trapper had hit the back trail before the fugitive hitched up his dogs and donned the familiar white parka that had become a symbol of reckless audacity along the Bitter River.

Then, when his matched team of white huskies finally set out, the Snow Hawk headed *southward*!

Through the arctic gloom sped the fleet white dogs. The Snow Hawk, instead of fleeing from Corporal Maxwell, was hastening to meet the man hunter.

There were many things about the Snow Hawk which Mandziak did not know, and the most surprising of these was the fact that Corporal Maxwell and the outlaw were not enemies but allies in a strange but common cause. When the Mounty reached Lonely Lake and proclaimed that he was on the Snow Hawk's trail, he knew perfectly well that someone would bring the warning to the young outlaw, wherever he was hidden. But it wasn't a warning. It was a summons.

The Snow Hawk, the white renegade of Bitter River, was hastening to meet the man who was said to have sworn to capture him, dead or alive.

Chapter 2:
A Date with Danger

His name was Dan Delaney, born and raised in the Yukon.

To the people of Bitter River country, he was the Snow Hawk, an outlaw.

Only Corporal Maxwell of the Mounted and Jean MacLean, of the trading post at Lonely Lake, knew the secret behind his presence in the Northland. They were the only ones who knew that Dan Delaney held an unofficial commission from Inspector Worth of the Mounted to track down a band of criminals hidden somewhere in the snow country.

Blackjack Adler and his gang!

Delaney had a personal interest in this quest. He knew that his own father, Matt Delaney, was held prisoner by Blackjack Adler's crew in some mountain hide-out. With the old man was Jean MacLean's brother, Doug. Doug and Matt were prospectors and partners, and the only reason they were still alive was the fact that they held the secret of a gold discovery in the Carcajou Creek country.

As Delaney sped toward Lonely Lake, he reviewed the twists of fate that had blocked his efforts to find Adler's hide-out. He had come close. There was a time when he nearly forced one of Adler's crew, a man named Bedell, to reveal the place. But Bedell had fallen to his death over a cliff. And there was Bedell's companion, a rogue named Ivan, who might have talked, but Ivan had escaped.

Jean MacLean and Maxwell were waiting for him when he reached the trading post that night.

"I knew someone would tell you I was here,"

smiled the Corporal. "But I expected to wait longer. Any trace of Adler?"

The Snow Hawk shook his head.

"No luck," he replied briefly. "I had a hunch that the gang was hidden in the Thunder Mountains. But I was wrong. There isn't a mountain trail I haven't accounted for. Do you know, corporal, I sometimes wonder if Adler *is* alive after all."

"He's alive, all right," growled Maxwell. "And he is just as smart as he was in his old pirate days. But how a gang can hide in the snow country without leaving a trail of some kind—it's beyond me."

"If Bedell had lived," said the Snow Hawk, "I might have made contact. So far as the Bitter River country is concerned, I'm a fugitive from justice, a man wanted for murder. But the plan is useless unless I can get in touch with some of Adler's men and convince them to play along with me."

"Bedell is dead," said Maxwell, "but the other fellow—Ivan, the man who escaped—is still alive."

"But where is he? Across the border by now, probably."

"No," declared the corporal quietly, "Ivan is not across the border."

Jean MacLean looked up quickly.

"You have traced Ivan?"

"Bedell and Ivan," the corporal told her, "came down from Adler's hide-out with the idea of stealing back from Young the money that had been paid over for supplies. But Ivan had already decided to desert Adler, so the pair divided the money and split up. Ivan escaped south. Bedell was killed, as you know, and his share of the money was found in his pockets. I brought the money in to headquarters. And that money has given us a clue."

The Snow Hawk learned forward, his eyes alert.

"A clue?"

"It was marked money!"

"Marked?"

"And some of that money has turned up?" asked Jean.

Maxwell nodded.

"A few of those marked bills have been reported from Portage d'Or, You've heard of the place—the toughest, roughest mining camp north of the border. The money turned up in a gambling joint. It's a good guess that Ivan is in Portage d'Or, spending those marked bills at the poker tables."

"Then," demanded Jean, "why don't you go to Portage d'Or and arrest Ivan?"

Corporal Maxwell shrugged.

"You forget," he answered, "that I do not know the fellow by sight. I might find him, of course, but I'm afraid I'd get precious little information out of him."

"It's my job," said the Snow Hawk. "I'll go."

"If I went down there and arrested Ivan," said Maxwell, "he would close up like a clam. But if you find him, I think you can persuade him to talk."

"I'll bargain with him. I'm the Snow Hawk. I'm wanted by the police. I'm looking for a hiding place. If he will tell me where to get in touch with Adler's gang, I'll forget what I know about him. If not—I'll do some talking about the affair at Blizzard Bluff. He'll listen to reason, I think, for he'll have nothing to lose and everything to gain."

"Exactly," agreed Maxwell. "But don't get the idea that it's going to be easy."

Jean MacLean looked anxiously at the corporal.

"Do you mean," she asked, "that there will be danger?"

"I mean just that," Maxwell replied. "This mining camp of Portage d'Or is a bad town and a tough town,

with the choicest collection of hard-boiled characters
you'll find between here and Winnipeg. It's probable
that Ivan has friends. He may figure that the safest
enemy is a dead enemy. Then again you'll have to re-
member that the Snow Hawk has a reputation as a bad
man. There are plenty of toughs around Portage d'Or
who would like to challenge that reputation. Think it
over, Dan."

The Snow Hawk grinned.

"But I would have a good chance of bluffing Ivan
and getting the dope on Blackjack Adler. I'm going,
corporal."

"You've got to bluff Ivan to a standstill. What's
more, you've got to bluff Portage d'Or at the same
time. There'll be danger, and plenty of it."

The Snow Hawk shrugged. Jean reached across the
table and put her hand on his arm.

"Isn't there some other way?" she asked. "You have
so many enemies among the fur thieves and whisky
traders and gamblers. Why, even the Mounted Police
haven't been told that you are anything but an outlaw."

There was a note of anxiety in her voice.

"I've got to go, Jean," he said gently, "How about
my dad—and your brother? Up there in Adler's
hide-out, somewhere in the north! This man Ivan
knows where they're hidden. And he's going to tell me.
I've got a date with Ivan."

Jean's eyes were troubled.

"No," she said slowly. "You have a date with danger. Perhaps with—"

"With what?"

"Death!" whispered the girl.

Chapter 3:
At Portage d'Or

Dan Delaney paused for a moment on the threshold of The Golden Hope, a long, low room that reeked with smoke and echoed with the clatter of chips, the rattle of dice, the buzz of a hundred voices. Here in this rough-and-ready mining camp, he was just another man in from the trail and anxious to sample what night life Portage d'Or had to offer.

As Delaney's eyes roved the motley crowd, as he scanned the faces of the players in search of the man named Ivan, he knew that he would have to move carefully. The men here could look after themselves. He saw mean faces, evil faces, hard faces. These were rough, hard-bitten men who had traveled far trails and seen odd corners of the world.

Delaney moved down into the shifting throng. He stood for a while watching one of the poker games. A genial, red-faced man who brushed against him looked up with a grin.

"Gambling?" he asked.

"After a while, perhaps," replied Delaney.

A tall, grotesque figure in a shabby overcoat, with a fur cap pulled down over his ears and dark glasses covering his eyes, shuffled around the table. In one hand he gripped a cane, in the other he clutched a tin cup.

"Bring yourselves a little luck, gents," he whined in a high-pitched voice. "Bring yourselves a little luck. Share up with the old blind man and you'll get a break."

One of the players tossed a quarter into the cup, drew three cards to fill his hand and flung them aside with a curse.

"He didn't say what kind of luck," a man guffawed.

The blind man went shuffling on his way, his cane tapping the floor. "Bring yourselves a little luck, gents," he whined. "Bring yourselves a little luck. Share up—"

Delaney moved on. He watched the crap game for a while, risked some money and lost. His mind, however, was not on the game. His eyes constantly scanned the shifting faces under the lamps.

It was while he stood there that he became aware that he was being watched. He could feel it.

Deliberately, he turned away from the table.

Beneath one of the overhanging lamps, Delaney saw a man dealing at a table against the wall.

The gambler was thin, with a bald head, hollow cheeks and a mouth like a blue slash across his hard face. He wore a green eyeshade that cast a livid pallor upon his features. And beyond the shelter of the eyeshade Delaney knew that the man's eyes were fixed on him.

Delaney stiffened. Under his breath he murmured a name:

"Baldy Kirk!"

Already he had encountered an enemy. He bit his lip with exasperation. Within an hour of his arrival in the camp he had met a man who knew him as the Snow Hawk.

The bald man arose abruptly from his chair, gestured curtly for another house man to take his place, and thrust his way through the crowd. He came toward Delaney, glowering.

"Baldy" Kirk was a professional gambler who did not believe in chance. He placed his faith in sure things, such as cold decks, marked cards and a highly-developed talent for dealing. It was while on expedition into the Bitter River country that Baldy Kirk had clashed with the Snow Hawk in the early winter. The upshot of the meeting had been that the Snow Hawk had thrust a gun against Baldy Kirk's stomach and neatly robbed the gambler of his winnings. The money had been returned to the trappers and rivermen whom Turk had swindled.

Baldy eyes, under the green shade were bitter with hostility as he approached.

"So!" he remarked. "The Snow Hawk!"

Delaney smiled calmly.

"Have we met?" he inquired.

"We've met," snapped Baldy Kirk. "Don't think I've forgotten it, either."

Delaney met Kirk's narrow eyes.

"So what?" he asked lazily.

Baldy's bald head gleamed in the light. The eyeshade gave his face a ghastly and sinister appearance. He extended a long, lean forefinger and poked Delaney in the chest.

"You're out of your territory, man," he rasped.

"I go where I please."

"I'm telling you," repeated Baldy, "you're out of your territory. If you want to stick around here, you'll square up our little account."

Delaney was still smiling.

"Have we a litttle account?"

"Fifteen hundred bucks! That's what you stole from me."

"And—"

"It won't do you any good to have this crowd know that the Snow Hawk is in the joint. Cough up, and I'll keep my mouth shut."

Delaney's smile faded. He leaned slightly forward.

"Try and get it, Baldy," he said distinctly, then turned his back on the gambler and lounged away.

The blind man shuffled past, his stick tap-tapping on the floor, droning his interminable: "Bring yourselves a little luck, gents. Bring yourselves a little luck—"

Delaney put a dollar in the cup.

"I'll take a dollar's worth," he said easily.

Delaney lounged over to the roulette layout and chose a position where he commanded a view of the whole room. He laid ten dollars on the red and appeared absorbed in the wheel, head down. But his eyes were watching the crowd.

He managed to pick out bald-head. The gambler was talking to a beefy, truculent giant who towered head and shoulders above everyone else in The Golden Hope. This man had bristly, close-cropped black hair and a thick jaw. Delaney studied the fellow and marked him as a bully.

"Who is the big guy talking to Baldy Kirk?" he asked quietly of the player at his left.

"You must be a stranger. That's Levits, the boss of Portage d'Or."

Delaney nodded. He had heard of Levits, a bad man with more than a local reputation. Levits was a noted rough-and-tumble fighter, and it was also said that he had notches on his gun.

Delaney sized up the fellow again, noticing that Levits had left Baldy Kirk and was now shouldering his way through the crowd toward the roulette table. So absorbed was Delaney that he had not been watching the wheel. His neighbor nudged him sharply.

"Going to let it ride again?"

Delaney looked down. A substantial heap of bills lay before him. Red had won four times running, and his winnings had automatically doubled. He grinned and reflected that perhaps the blind man had brought him luck after all.

"Let it ride," he said.

He could see Levits drawing closer. The blind man, making his way through the crowd, happened to blunder directly into the big man's path, stumbled against him. Levits' lips drew back in a snarl; he swung a mighty arm, and the blind man went staggering back into the crowd, reeled and sprawled on the floor, coins tinkling as they were flung from his upturned cup.

Delaney bit his lip. In the next moment, Levits had shouldered into a place at his side. The wheel was spinning. The dancing ball whirled and tumbled.

"Red wins!"

Delaney's original bet had grown to three hundred and twenty dollars. Levits jostled roughly against him, breathing heavily. Delaney reached for his money.

"Lost your nerve?" demanded Levits in an ugly tone.

Delaney knew that he was there for the express purpose of picking a fight, urged on by Baldy Kirk. He saw, too, that a crowd was gathering about the roulette table, and he sensed a change in the atmosphere of The Golden Hope. He looked Levits in the eye.

"No," he said. "I've had enough."

Levits thick lips curled back from yellow teeth.

"Thought so," he grunted. "It takes more nerve than you've got to play the red again."

By way of reply Delaney put the wad of bills down beside the layout.

"A side bet," he said softly, "on the red."

A little gasp went up from the crowd. Levits had expected anything but that. Delaney was putting it up to him, making a personal issue of the matter. Levits would have to risk more than three hundred dollars if he cared to test the Snow Hawk's nerve.

A wiry little man beyond the table drawled:

"He's calling you, Levits! Put up or shut up!"

Levits had stepped into his own trap. If he backed down now, his prestige in Portage d'Or would be shattered. With a grunt he thrust his hand into his pocket and drew out a heavy roll of bills.

"On the black!" he growled.

Delaney smiled. He did not look at Levits. Instead, his eyes were scanning the faces of the mob jammed about the table.

The wheel was spinning. Delaney paid no attention. For one face seemed fairly to leap out of the crowd.

Back under one of the green-shaded lights he saw a familiar, bearded face. He felt a thrill of excitement, a tightening of the nerves. For that swarthy, flattish face brought back in a swift rush of memory the scene in the cabin at Blizzard Bluff when Young, the trader, lay dead and the two outlaws from Blackjack Adler's camp held command.

It was the face of Ivan!

Delaney fought down a wild impulse to plunge from the table and thrust his way through the crowd.

Here was the man he sought, not ten feet away. In the dead silence that overhung the hall Delaney could hear the soft clicking of the wheel, the tense breathing of the watchers. But he dared not move until this test of nerve was finished.

The wheel was running down. It came to a stop. The ball jumped, stumbled and clicked smartly into a red slot. "Red wins!"

Red had won six times running. Delaney coolly picked up Black Levits' money, stacked it in a heap with his own, and flicked his thumb toward the pile of bills.

"Another side bet," he said, "on the red!"

Oaths and murmurs of astonishment came from the crowd.

There was no question of the Snow Hawk's nerve now. He was betting more than six hundred dollars on a color that had already had a run of six. The question now was whether Levits dared take him up.

Levits face was dark with anger. He looked up, seeking Baldy Kirk, beckoned the gambler toward him. They had a brief conference. Levits was broke, wanted Baldy to stake him. A wad of bills changed hands, and Levits sullenly planked the money down beside the layout.

"I'm taking it," he said thickly.

The wheel spun again. Delaney was watching Ivan. He was bound to remain where he was until this strange clash with Levits was settled, but in the meantime he did not want to lose sight of Ivan for an instant. And Ivan recognized him, he knew. The man's eyes were fixed on him in terrified fascination.

The wheel whirled steadily, the ball rolling and dancing. Levits' heavy face wore a scowl. Delaney did not care whether he won or not. It was improbable that red would win again, but at least he had won the respect of The Golden Hope.

The wheel ran down—came to a clicking stop—

A shout went up.

"Zero!"

Delaney looked down. The ball was in the white slot. Had the bets been on the table, the house would have won. As it was, the issue was still unsettled.

The wheel spun again. When he looked up, he could not see Ivan. After a while he saw a head moving at the edge of the crowd.

His quarry was going toward the door. Delaney's hands clenched with anxiety. The wheel seemed to be spinning interminably. The man was having trouble shoving his way through the mob at the back of the room. The ball skittered and hopped—the wheel was spinning more slowly now.

And this time, when it came to a stop, there was no shout. Merely a great incredulous gasp. Dan had won again, for the seventh time in succession.

Delaney looked down, his face impassive. He picked up the money and put it into his pocket. A babel of talk broke out. People were crowding about him. Levits was talking loudly to Baldy Kirk, obviously trying to persuade him to put up the twelve hundred and eighty dollars that would be necessary to cover another bet.

Delaney shouldered his way through the crowd, elbowing people right and left. He overtook Ivan just as the man was opening the door. His arm shot out, and his fingers clamped over Ivan's wrist.

"I want to talk to you!" he said quietly.

Ivan's eyes shifted, he licked his lips nvervously.

"What about?" he muttered.

Delaney urged him toward the door.

"Come along!"

Ivan held back.

"If you've got anything to say to me," he grumbled defiantly, "you can say it here."

Delaney's eyes were like flecks of ice.

"You're coming with me!" he said softly.

In the next instant, a huge hand gripped Delaney's shoulder and swung him around. A menacing voice snarled:

"Leave the guy alone!"

Delaney looked into the ugly, wrathful face of Levits. The bully was glad for any excuse that would help him restore his lost prestige and settle once and for all the issue between himself and the Snow Hawk.

"He's coming with me!" snapped Delaney.

Levits' eyes gleamed. This was what he wanted. Ponderously, his left arm swung, driving directly for Delaney's face.

Chapter 4:
A Clash with Levits

Dan Delaney had been heavyweight champion of his college in his senior year.

His head shifted a fraction of an inch as Levits fist swung with the slow, terrific force of a grizzly's paw. The blow missed, and the next instant Delaney was inside his opponent's guard.

A slashing left uppercut caught Levits fairly on the jaw. It was a jolting, choppy blow that made the big man's teeth rattle, and it was followed by a right that sent him back on his heels, glassy-eyed.

Levits clinched while his head cleared, and Delaney found it impossible to shake off the man's great weight, break free of those heavy, encircling arms.

Levits was snarling low in his throat, like an animal. Delaney beat a crashing tattoo against the big fellow's ribs, but he might have been battering a stone pillar. Then Levits began to use some of his tricks.

A knee came up, jammed hard against Delaney's belly. An agonizing pain shot through his body. He wilted with agony.

Levits head went down, then rose with sudden force as he tried to butt Delaney beneath the chin. Delaney's head instinctively rolled, and the deadly thrust lost most of its effect. Had it landed squarely, it would have cost Delaney his senses and most of his teeth; as it was, he was half stunned by the glancing blow against the side of his jaw. An elbow was rammed savagely against his throat. Levits' huge fingers clawed at his face, a brutal thumb gouging, seeking his eyes.

The two men stumbled furiously among the tables as Delaney tried to drive Levits back, tried to break free

of that deadly embrace. Levits twisted one leg around
Dan's thigh, kicked viciously at the back of his ankle.
The heavy boot protected Delaney, and as he swung
around he got his face clear of Levits' groping fingers.
He lowered his head, buried it in his opponent's chest
and by sheer force bullied the other man backward.
They crashed into one of the poker tables. It went over
with a great clatter of chips. Delaney felt himself flung
around, shaken mercilessly. Again Levits tried to butt
him in the face; again he dodged.

That one experience had been enough. Delaney
stayed away from the huge, flailing arms, but he lashed
out a left that caught Levits' face and drew blood,
danced in and drove a pile-driver punch to the giant's
stomach.

Levits gasped. His mouth opened and shut as he
tried to get breath. Delaney swept around him, crouching and weaving, ducked under one sweeping blow that
would have driven him halfway across the room had it
landed, and then came in fast for a terrific smash to the
face and another to the side of the head.

Levits sagged. He was driven back, his head lolling.
Delaney went after him relentlessly. Dan feinted, drew
Levits toward him, dodged another ponderous swing,
and then came in as Levits was off-balance.

A looping left caught the giant on the jaw. Delaney
stepped in and slammed a crushing right that dropped
the big man in his tracks.

As Levits crashed to the floor on his haunches, Delaney stood there crouching, fists clenched, watching the
crowd. He could see Baldy Kirk, saw the glowering and
hostile faces of Levits' friends.

As for Levits, he was sprawled on his back. He struggled up, one hand wrenching at his belt.

A revolver appeared in Levits' hand. Delaney's
arm flashed down and he dodged as the revolver spat

flame and a bullet fanned his cheek. His own gun was out in an instant.

Delaney backed away, fired deliberately at Levits' blazing weapon. Levits' gun spun in the air and crashed to the floor as the man yelled with pain.

Delaney backed to the door. His revolver covered the ring of staring faces in The Golden Hope. Swiftly he scanned all those hard, shadowy countenances under the lights. But there was no sign of Ivan.

"Does anyone else want to make a reputation for himself?" he demanded.

No one spoke. He picked out Baldy from the crowd:

"You can tell Ivan," snapped Delaney, "that I'm staying at Prospector's Hotel and that he had better come to see me there, if he wants to keep out of trouble!"

This was not only a warning to Ivan, who would certainly receive the message. It was a flat challenge to Baldy Kirk, to Levits and anyone else who might be tempted to take the Snow Hawk's measure. He was not running away. He was telling them where he could be found.

Delaney reached back, yanked open the door. With gun still leveled, he stepped back against the threshold out into the snow. Then he slammed the door and strode away into the night.

Delaney's mouth was bitter with disappointment as he walked down the street back toward the shabby hotel. For all his victory over Levits, he knew that the obstacles against him had been doubled.

Through no fault of his own, the affair had been badly bungled. Baldy Kirk and Levits would not take their defeat lying down. Every moment he remained in the camp would be fraught with danger. His identity was known, he had made dangerous enemies, and every move he made would be watched from now on.

Above all, he had lost Ivan.

"There will be blood on the moon before I get out of this town," he muttered.

The defeat of Levits created a sensation in The Golden Hope. The swarthy giant had ruled the roost in Portage d'Or since the early days of the camp. Now, as the games were resumed under the green-shaded lights, there was but one topic of conversation, one undercurrent to the heavy buzz of excited talk.

The Snow Hawk had given Levits a three-way trimming. He had called Levits' bluff and taken his money at the wheel. He had beaten him to the punch and given him an artistic trouncing. Then, to top it all, he had beaten Levits to the draw.

"Levits bit off plenty more than he could chew when he tangled with that guy!" declared a leather-faced old-timer, hitching his chair up to one of the poker tables again. "He'll never live this down."

"Not unless he does something," grunted another player quietly.

The old-timer nodded.

"Yeah," he said. "That's the point. What's Levits going to do about it?"

That was the question that hung over The Golden Hope. What was Levits going to do about it?

And that, precisely, was the question Baldy Kirk was putting to Levits at the moment. In one of the back rooms, the gambler tied a bandage about Levits' hand. At the table sat Ivan, his fingers nervously drumming the woodwork.

"A fine mess you made of it!" snarled Baldy. "I told you to pick a fight with that guy and beat him!"

"Why didn't you do it yourself?" growled Levits. "I can lick any man living in a rough-and-tumble, but that fellow didn't give me a chance. He's a professional."

"He was just too smart for you. If you're going to let

him get away with this, you might as well pull out of Portage d'Or."

"He's not going to get away with it!"

"You try to show him up—and what happens? He takes twelve hundred bucks off us, smears your face all over your ears, and gives you a handful of hot lead."

The words stung. Levits' face was flushed with humiliation and hatred. With his good hand he drew his revolver and clumped it on the table.

"He's not going to get away with it!" he shouted. "What has this Snow Hawk got on you?"

A scowl passed over Ivan's sinister face.

"Plenty!"

Baldy studied Ivan silently. He knew very little about the man. Nobody knew anything about Ivan, except that he had money, that he gambled freely, and that he had something on his conscience.

"You'll feel safer if he's out of the way," Baldy suggested.

Ivan nodded.

"One of us has got to get out of town."

"Nobody is leaving town. Not alive," said Baldy Kirk.

"I'll play with you," declared Ivan. "What have you got in mind?"

Baldy Kirk frowned.

"This Snow Hawk," he said, "wanted to talk to you. He didn't draw on you."

"He wants some information," muttered Ivan.

"Then," snapped Baldy Kirk, rapping his knuckles on the table, "he'll get his information."

Ivan shook his head fearfully.

"Not from me. It's as much as my neck is worth."

Baldy snorted.

"Don't be a fool! He'll never live to use it."

The light shone on Baldy Kirk's gleaming skull, his

shrewd, scheming face. It cast shadows on Ivan's face and on Black Levits' bruised features.

"He owes me fifteen hundred bucks that he stole from me early this winter," declared Baldy Kirk. "And he's got twelve hundred bucks in his pocket right now." He looked directly at Levits. "You borrowed six hundred of that from me, and unless you can get it back, you're going to pay me."

"I'll get it back."

"You will if you do as I say."

Baldy Kirk talked, emphasizing his remarks by rapping the table sharply with his bony knuckles.

Outside the room, at the crowded tables of The Golden Hope, the roulette wheel whirred, the dice rattled, the chips clattered and the cards were shuffled. But the atmosphere had altered. There was suspense in the air.

What was Levits going to do about it?

At the door of the little room where Baldy Kirk was talking slowly and deliberately to Ivan and Levits stood the blind man. His cup was held out pleadingly. Once in a while he whined:

"Bring yourselves a little luck, gents. Help the poor old blind man—"

Chapter 5:
The Trap

Dan Delaney went back to the ramshackle frame building known as The Prospector's Hotel, but he did not go up to his room. Instead, he sat down in a chair beside the stove and waited.

Ivan would get his message. He knew that. And he was fairly confident that Ivan would respond to it. Ivan had been a member of Blackjack Adler's gang, which indicated that he had a criminal record. The Snow Hawk could set the police on his trail at a word. Ivan would come to bargain with him.

"The question is this," said Delaney to himself: "who will come here first? Levits or Ivan?"

Under cover of his coat, he reloaded his gun. He did not believe in taking chances.

The door opened, and an unhealthy looking young man with squinty eyes, a sharp nose and a bluish skin sidled into the hotel. He darted a swift glance at Delaney, then came over and sat down in the vacant chair beside him. Delaney did not speak. The newcomer extracted a package of cigarettes and thrust one between his lips. It waggled nervously.

"Ivan wants to see you," muttered the young man with the squint.

Delaney shrugged. "What's stopping him?"

The other flicked a match on his thumb nail and lit the cigarette. "He sent a note."

Delaney extended his hand. "Let's have it."

The other gave him a crumpled bit of dirty paper. Delaney unfolded it. The message was written in smudgy pencil.

This guy will show you were I live. I don't want

31

any trouble with you for I know you can make trouble for me. Let bygones be bygones and I will tell you what you want to know. I will wait here until you come.

IVAN

Delaney crumpled up the note and thrust it into his pocket. The youth stood up expectantly. Delaney did not move.

"Well, are you coming?"

Delaney shook his head. "No."

"Why not?"

"I'm not running after him. If he wants to see me, he can find me here."

The youth looked puzzled. "But he can't come out. He said he'd wait for you. Don't you want to see him?"

"Not particularly," bluffed Delaney. "You go back and tell Ivan that I'm pulling out of town in half an hour. If he wants to see me, he'd better move fast."

The youth looked at him uncertainly.

"But he doesn't want to come here to talk to you."

"I don't care what he wants," rasped Delaney. "He'll do what I want. Get that? He'll come here, or it will be the worse for him. Get out of here and tell him that."

The moment the messenger was out the door, Delaney got up. He wanted to see Ivan, but not so badly that he cared to walk into a trap. And this might be a snare set for him. He opened the door cautiously and lounged in the entrance, looking down the street. He could see the squint-eyed youth walking hurriedly off through the snow. The boy crossed the road and went down the first side street to the left. He did not look back.

Delaney strode in pursuit. At the corner he caught sight of him again, heading down the street toward the

shacks and cabins that trailed off toward the outskirts
of Portage d'Or. Delaney kept well in the shadows,
holding close to the buildings that flanked the street.

The road sloped toward a hillside topped by the
gaunt structure of a shaft house. At the foot of the hill
the village ended, terminating in a few straggling cabins
set far apart in the snow. The road gave way to a trail.
Delaney halted in the shadow of a store with a false
front and watched the dark figure of the messenger.

The youth made his way up the trail toward the last
of the cabins. The night was clear, and Delaney could
see him distinctly even at that distance. A splotch of
light fell across the snow as a door was opened. The
messenger went inside.

"Now," he said grimly, "I'll take a look."

First of all, however, Delaney took the wad of
money he had won in The Golden Hope from his
pocket. He knew very well that Baldy Kirk would
make at least one effort to prevent him from taking that
money out of the camp.

Delaney wrapped the bills in his bandana and stowed
the bundle in the snow beside the wall of the store.
Carefully he thrust snow over the hiding place so that
to the casual eye there was no sign of a cache.

The money was his, and he had won it fairly. The
expenses in connection with his long search for his father had been heavy, and in recent weeks he had been
low in funds. This money would come in handy.

Then he strode out along the trail toward the cabin
at the foot of the hill.

There was a light in the solitary window, and he
watched carefully for any shadow upon the glass. But
apparently the inmates of the place were not suspicious,
and he was satisfied that his approach was unobserved.

Delaney left the trail as he came near the cabin and
circled around to the side. He drew close to the window

on hands and knees. He could hear a low murmur of voices. Cautiously he raised himself toward the sill and peered through the bleary glass.

The cabin was small and untidy, illuminated by a guttering kerosene lamp. Ivan, black-bearded and somber, sat at a wooden table. In the middle of the room stood Levits, his thumbs hooked in his belt. Beside the stove sat the squint-eyed youth.

"You're a fine guy to send out," grumbled Levits. "Why didn't you talk to him? He didn't figure there was anything wrong, did he?"

"No, it wasn't that. He was just stubborn. He said Ivan had to come to him. What could I do?"

"I told you this guy was smart," said Ivan morosely. "How did he track me down? I don't know. But he did it. You aren't going to get him just by sending for him."

"Then we'll go after him," snarled Levits. "What else did he say, Sam?"

"He said to tell Ivan he'd wait half an hour and then he was going to pull out of town."

Ivan shifted nervously in his chair.

"I guess I'd better go and talk to him. I can't take any chances."

"You're staying here," Levits grunted. "We'll have to wait until Baldy shows up. Then we'll figure out a scheme."

Delaney's mouth tightened. He dropped beneath the level of the window and looked back down the trail. Sure enough, a dark figure was just emerging from the shadowy huddle of shacks at the end of the distant gloomy street.

Baldy Kirk! If it had not been for Levits' remark, Delaney would have remained at the window, to be caught flatfooted by the gambler approaching silently through the snow.

He crept along the side of the cabin, pressing close to the logs, and went around to the back. There he crouched, watching the figure trudging up the trail.

Baldy Kirk came closer, passed out of Delaney's line of vision as he strode up to the front of the cabin. A moment later Delaney heard the door open and shut.

He crept back to the window and raised himself slightly. He could see Baldy confronting the others.

"Haven't you gone yet, Sam?" he asked.

"I'm back," grumbled Sam. "He wouldn't fall for it."

Baldy shrugged. He went over to Levits and drew him to one side. They whispered for a moment, and then Levits lounged over to the stove.

"I think I'd better go and talk to him myself," Ivan muttered. "I'm taking the chances. If he goes and starts shooting off his mouth to a cop, where will I be?"

"Yeah," sneered Baldy. "That's what I'd like to know. Where *will* you be? Behind bars?"

He watched Ivan narrowly. Ivan blinked and licked his lips. The shot had told.

"I thought so," said Baldy Kirk. "Well, you'd better play along with us, or somebody else may give the cops an earful."

"Aren't I playing with you?" demanded Ivan.

"You are, whether you like it or not. Look here, Sam. What did he say when you gave him the note? Why wouldn't he come?"

Sam repeated his story. Levits opened the back door.

"I've got to go out for a minute," he said.

Delaney was away from the window in a flash. He backed along the side of the cabin, gun in hand, reached the corner and waited.

He heard Levits' footsteps crunching in the snow.

Delaney edged around the corner. He was now at the front of the building. He crouched there, watching, but Levits did not come around to the side. Then Delaney heard a creak, the noisy rasp of a frosted hinge. He looked back over his shoulder, and a stream of light fell full upon his startled face as the door was flung violently open.

A heavy figure plunged across the threshold. Delaney whirled, but he had made no more than a half turn before Baldy Kirk crashed into him.

The butt of a revolver raked Delaney's forehead and stunned him for a moment, but he had managed instinctively to brace himself for the impact of Baldy's body, and he was not knocked off his feet.

Kirk pulled him back into the snow, slogged at him with the gun, battering him about the head and shoulders, but Delaney grappled with him and brought up his own gun.

A terrific smash, however, knocked the weapon out of his grasp, and it fell into the snow. He let go with a left-hand swing that caught Kirk in the face and drove the gambler back on his heels.

Delaney saw another figure surging through the doorway. And then another. Ivan and Sam were in the fracas now.

They both rushed him. He turned and laced out a straight-arm jolt that nailed the squint-eyed youth in the throat and turned him halfway around, gagging. Baldy Kirk leaped in again, striking out with the revolver, and Ivan had him by the waist, trying to knock him off his feet.

Delaney dodged the gun, jammed Ivan in the face with a vicious thrust of his elbow and broke free. He wheeled and stumbled toward the side of the cabin.

A gigantic figure loomed before him. It was Levits. The big man plunged and brought Delaney down by sheer weight, knocked him into the deep snow.

In the next moment they were all upon him, like a

pack of wolves. Delaney was beaten, kicked and pummeled, dragged to his feet and hustled roughly into the cabin.

The squint-eyed youth produced a length of rope; Delaney's arms were bound tightly behind him, and he was flung into a chair. There, with his face hard and defiant, he faced his four captors.

"Smart work!" said Baldy. "Smart work all around." His grin was sinister. "You outsmarted yourself, Mr. Snow Hawk."

Delaney said nothing. He had blundered directly into the trap, knowing it was a trap. And now the lamplight shone on four merciless faces.

"You thought you were pretty cagey when you told Sam you wouldn't come, and then shadowed him. But I was cagey too," bragged the gambler. "Well!" he snorted contemptuously. "I could see your head against that window three hundred yards away. You shadowed Sam. I shadowed you. And here we are."

Delaney was wondering why he had not been shot down in the fight at the front of the cabin. Baldy Kirk had been careful to use his gun only as a club. Not a shot had been fired.

Now he was enlightened. For Levits strode over and roughly went through his pockets.

"No?" said Baldy.

Levits shook his head. He drew back and struck Delaney across the mouth with the back of his hand. The blow split Delaney's lips and drew a trickle of blood.

"Where's that money?" snarled Levits.

Delaney laughed.

"Where you'll never get it!"

Levits cursed and struck him again.

"It won't do you any good, Snow Hawk," rasped Baldy Kirk, "for you're not going to live to spend it!"

Chapter 6:
The Blind Man

Ivan nodded. "Yes," he said, "this Snow Hawk must die. He is dangerous to me—to all of us."

"Hear that?" barked Baldy Kirk, looking at Delaney. "You're all washed up. You know why. First of all, you've got something on Ivan. What it is, I don't know, but it must be plenty. Second—you stole fifteen hundred bucks from me, and you won't pay up. In my game, the guy who won't pay up is committing suicide, and that's what you've done. Third—you beat up Levits and shot him in the hand. Fourth, maybe you don't know that you've wrecked the booze racket in the Bitter River country. Maybe you don't know that the boys who control that racket have a standing price of five thousand bucks on your head. The guy who knocks off the Snow Hawk gets five thousand bucks on the line, and no questions asked."

This was news to Delaney, but he was not surprised.

"Well, then," he snapped contemptuously, "get it over with. Go ahead and shoot. There are four of you. Do the job yourself, Baldy. You'd like to. I dare you. I dare you to take a chance on your gang sticking with you. You know that every one of them would squeal the moment he got into a jam."

Baldy's eyes flickered. He knew that this was true.

"Go ahead, Levits," continued Delaney. "*You* do it. Baldy will stick by you. If he ever breaks with you, he'll never think of double-crossing you. Not for a minute."

Then he looked at Sam.

"Come on, Squint-eye. Why don't you do it? They'll all stand behind you. If you're caught, they'll all go on the witness stand—against you. You can depend on them!"

His contemptuous eyes fell on Ivan.

"Sam checks out. It's up to you, Ivan. They're all friends of yours. It wouldn't matter to them if they had a little thing like murder on you. You can trust them."

Delaney had introduced a new element—that of mutual fear and suspicion. He had struck at their one weakness—the fact that not one of them would trust another.

Baldy Kirk rubbed his chin craftily.

"But we're not letting you get away with that money," he said.

"I'll make a deal with you. Take the money and let me go."

Baldy and Levits drew to one side and conferred in whispers. Ivan looked up, frowning.

"Nothing doing!" he said. "Where do I get off?"

But Kirk looked up.

"Will you do the job?" he said pointedly.

Ivan hesitated, looked at Kirk's shifty eyes, at the weak countenance of Sam, at Levits' glowering face.

"No!" he said flatly.

"You see," replied Kirk, with a helpless gesture, "he hit the nail on the head. Where's the dough, Snow Hawk?"

"In the hotel safe. Cut these ropes, and I'll go down with you and hand it over."

Kirk grinned.

"Do I look stupid? You'll write a note ordering the clerk to hand over the coin. That's what you'll do. You'll put your room key in the note so the clerk will know everything is okay. When we have the money, we'll let you go, but not before. That's the way I do business."

Delaney looked crestfallen. Baldy went over to a shelf and came back with a small pad of paper and a pencil. He untied the ropes that bound Delaney's arms.

Levits covered Delaney with a gun. He had to hold the revolver in his left hand.

Delaney took the pencil and wrote: "Please give bearer envelope I turned over to you for safe keeping tonight." He signed it: "James Green," and tossed his room key onto the table before him.

Baldy Kirk read the note carefully. "Is that your real name?" he asked.

Delaney laughed scornfully.

"It's the name I signed on the register."

Kirk gave the note and the key to Sam.

"Get down to the hotel and collect," he snapped. "And God help you if you forget to come back."

Sam vanished. Baldy twisted Delaney's arms behind his back again and tied him up once more. But this time Delaney held his arms rigid, crooked at the elbows.

"What's the idea?" he demanded. "Why are you tying me up if you're going to let me go when Sam comes back?"

His ruse with the note was only a gamble. He was not registered at the hotel under the name of James Green, and he had left no envelope with the clerk. It was his hope that when Sam presented the note and the key, the discrepancies might arouse so much suspicion that the clerk would investigate. It would certainly be known in the hotel by now that the man who held the key to No. 14 was the Snow Hawk.

Baldy showed his teeth in a triumphant grin.

"We're not going to let you go when Sam comes back," he said. Levits uttered a harsh laugh.

"I might have known!" said Delaney bitterly.

"You hit it right," said Baldy, "when you figured we wouldn't knock you off if it had to be a single-handed job. But you were wrong when you thought you were springing a new idea on us. Don't you give me credit for any brains? I had to kid you into thinking I fell for it, so you'd make your little deal and cough up the money."

He looked at Ivan and Levits for approval of his shrewdness. A slow smile spread over Ivan's face, and he slapped his knee. Levits grunted admiringly.

"No getting away from it, Baldy," he said. "You're always about three jumps ahead."

"And as for thinking you can buy us out for a measly twelve hundred bucks," went on Baldy complacently, "you were kidding yourself there, too. You're washed up, Snow Hawk. We're going through with this—*but we're going through with it together!*"

Ivan leaned forward, frowning.

"Up in Alaska," continued Baldy deliberately, "they had a way of dealing with thieves. If a man robbed a food cache and was caught at it, this is what happened to him. His hands were tied behind his back and he was turned loose in the mountains. Over his shoulders was a sign reading: 'This is a thief. Pass him along.' And he was passed along until he dropped. No one would even think of taking him in."

His lank forefinger tapped the table.

"That's how you're going out, Snow Hawk. It's twenty-five degrees below zero right now, and it'll be lower before morning. Ivan and Levits and Sam and I are going to take you up into the hills and turn you loose, with your hands tied and a blindfold over your eyes so you won't find your way back to town in time to save yourself from freezing. And when they find your body, stiff as a board, there will be a sign on your back reading: 'This is the Snow Hawk.'"

Delaney's face was grim and expressionless.

"That," said Baldy, "will square me for that fifteen hundred bucks you stole. It will square Levits for what you did to him tonight. And it will square Ivan for what you *might* do to him if you stayed alive."

There was dead silence.

Delaney's eyes were half closed. This was the end of the Snow Hawk's trail. He pictured the rocky, snow-covered slopes, the steep cliffs, the treacherous defiles—he saw a bound and blinded figure staggering through the night—zero weather, with cold that froze the blood.

He saw, too, the cozy living room of the trading post at Lonely Lake, saw the friendly faces of Corporal Maxwell and Jean MacLean. He heard again her frightened words: "You have a date with danger. Perhaps with death!"

She had been right. He had kept his date with danger, and now he was to keep a date with death. His long search for his father would come to a futile and inglorious end among the icy rocks that looked down on Portage d'Or.

Delaney braced his shoulders and met Baldy Kirk's hard, malicious gaze.

"Well?" he snapped. "Why are you waiting? Get it over with."

"There's no hurry," replied Kirk. "We'll wait until Sam comes back."

A sharp, startling sound echoed through the cabin!

Ivan leaped to his feet, with a terrified oath. Levits swung around, snatching up his gun from the table. Baldy whirled to face the door, and a revolver appeared like magic in his hand. Everyone stared at the door, their bodies tense.

For the sound had been a knock, sharp and emphatic. Now it was repeated. Three distinct, clamorous knocks!

"Who's there?" demanded Baldy.

"It's only me," whined a curious, muffled voice. "Let me in, whoever you are. I've lost my way. I'm half frozen."

Baldy advanced cautiously to the door, gun ready.

"It's that blind guy," he muttered. "Now, how on earth did he get out here?"

He thrust back the bolt, opened the door a trifle. They saw the butt of a stout wooden stick grope through the opening, distinguished a gloomy shape beyond.

"What do you want?" demanded Baldy roughly.

The blind man forced his way into the cabin and stood there in his long, shabby coat, the stick gripped tightly in his hand, the lamplight shining on his black spectacles.

"Where am I, sir?" he whined. "I've lost my way. I've been wandering knee-deep in snow for the past half hour. I was afraid I'd freeze to death. Where am I?"

The moment the blind man crossed the threshold, Levits had swung around behind Delaney's chair, snatched a heavy sweater from the wall and thrust it in Delaney's face. He held it there in both hands, and Delaney was effectively gagged.

"You're way off course, Gilstrom," said Baldy. He kept the door open. The lamp guttered. "I'll put you back on the trail. The street isn't far."

"You know my name?" said the visitor, his head on one side. "Your voice is familiar. Ah, yes—that gambling place—"

"Well, I'm busy just now. It won't take you long to get back to the street again."

"I'm very cold," muttered Gilstrom.

Baldy had thrust his revolver back into his belt. Ivan, with a curious expression in his sinister eyes, was leaning across the table, staring at Gilstrom. The blind man thrust his stick beneath his arm and jammed his hands into his coat pockets.

"I'm half frozen," he whined. "If you could let me warm myself at your fire—"

"I tell you I'm busy!" rasped Baldy, getting angry. "Beat it out of here before—"

The blind man did a most astonishing thing. His hand leaped from his pockets, gripping a heavy revolver. The gun was trained on Baldy Kirk.

"Get them up!" ordered Gilstrom, in a voice like the clang of steel.

They were paralyzed with amazement. Baldy's eyes literally bulged from his head. Ivan's mouth fell open; he seemed dazed. Levits' hand tightened convulsively on the sweater that nearly covered Delaney's face.

"You can't see!" shouted Kirk.

And his hands dropped toward his gun. The revolver blazed instantly, and a bullet plucked a fragment of cloth from Baldy Kirk's sleeve. The gambler's arms shot about his head instantly.

"No?" said Gilstrom. "Make another try for your gun, and you'll find out how blind I am!"

He lowered his head, brushed his face against one arm, and the black spectacles fell to the floor. He gestured curtly with the gun.

"Go on over there beside the table!" he barked at Levits.

The big man, raising his arms slowly, reluctantly obeyed. Not a man in the room took his eyes off Gilstrom.

"What's the idea?" gasped Baldy in a husky voice.

Gilstrom nodded toward Ivan.

"I want you!" he snapped. Then he looked at Delaney. "And you! Under arrest, the pair of you."

"A cop!" blurted Levits.

"You're wanted for murder and robbery," Gilstrom said curtly to Ivan. "As for you," he said to Delaney, "you're the Snow Hawk, and that's enough. Mounted Police headquarters want you both!"

Chapter 7:
An Inferno

Delaney felt an insane desire to yell with laughter. The utter amazement of his captors was the angry astonishment of men who realize that they have been tricked and defeated simply and completely. Even yet they could not credit the situation.

They could not believe that this fake blind man, groping his way around The Golden Hope with tin cup and cane, was a Mounty in disguise. To him, the Snow Hawk was a fugitive from justice, in the same class as Ivan.

"I don't know what's been going on here," snapped Gilstrom, the revolvers gripped steadily in his hands, "but it doesn't look good. I'm warning you, Kirk—and you, Levits—that we'll be watching you from now on."

To Delaney he said:

"Well, Snow Hawk! We've caught up with you at last. Maybe I'm doing you a favor in taking you out of here. Maybe not. You have plenty to answer for when you get to headquarters."

"You don't know the half of it," Delaney told him.

"Yeah? Well, you won't feel so funny when you're cooling your heels in a cell." His eyes turned on Ivan. "You know why you're wanted, don't you?"

Ivan nodded slowly.

"Yes," he said, in a thick, unnatural voice. "I know why you want me." His voice rose to a scream. "It's murder, that's what it is! Just plain murder!" He turned to Baldy and Levits. "This guy!" he yelled, pointing a trembling finger at Gilstrom. "I know him! I know why he's here! Why, he's a—"

A sudden clatter of the latch, and then the door was

flung open. Gilstrom whirled around. Baldy took a step forward. There on the threshold stood Sam, the squint-eyed youth.

"He was lying!" yelped Sam. "The clerk said there wasn't an envelope—"

And then the words died in his throat. His mouth gaped as Gilstrom swung toward him, covering him with one gun, the other weapon covering the others in the room.

"Get in here!" shouted Gilstrom. "Get over there with the others!"

Sam's arrival, however, had put Gilstrom in a bad position. He tried to get back toward the wall so that his gun would still command the entire cabin. But Ivan, halfway to his feet, grabbed the moment in which he was uncovered.

His arm made a mighty sweep; he snatched up the lamp and hurled it with all his force. It described a bright, flaming arc across the cabin, crashed against the wall behind Gilstrom, and exploded in a sharp and violent sheet of flame.

Gilstrom's gun roared. The cabin was plunged into instant confusion, with the leaping figures of men swinging like phantoms through the eerie light.

Delaney leaped to his feet, struggling to free himself from the chair in which he was tied. When he had been bound for the second time, the ruse of holding his arms rigid had given the rope some slack, and he had been working at them steadily and unobtrusively. Now he shook furiously at his bonds, flung himself around, felt the ropes give. They were tied beneath his arms and knotted around the back of the chair. He got clear to the extent that the chair swung around in front of him, ropes dangling, and he grabbed the back of it and lifted it high.

He saw Levits looming down on him. Delaney twisted and swung.

The chair crashed against Levits and the big man staggered back with a yell. Through the flickering flames that were now rising along the end wall of the cabin, he saw Ivan and Baldy in a heap, with Gilstrom beneath, while Sam capered around and bleated with terror.

Delaney plunged toward them, wrestled the chair over his head and shook the ropes free of his arms.

Baldy sprang up, gun in hand. Delaney swung the chair again. It smashed down on Baldy's arm. The revolver leaped in the air. Baldy Kirk sprang at him.

Ivan and Gilstrom were struggling in front of the door. Delaney saw Ivan's arm rise and fall. Gilstrom tumbled back in a heap.

Baldy plunged and Delaney was nearly knocked off his feet. He flung the chair aside, for it was useless at close quarters, and rocked Baldy with a blow to the side of his head.

A gun blazed somewhere, and Delaney saw Ivan crouching, firing at him. The bullet whistled past his head.

Delaney wrestled Baldy away from him and drove a left that sent the gambler reeling across the cabin. Delaney dove sideways, his hand groping for the gun he had knocked from Baldy Kirk's grasp.

The roar and crackle of flames increased. The heat became oppressive. Ivan's gun blazed again, but Delaney lunged flat on the floor as he saw the revolver he sought, and the bullet passed over him.

Gilstrom, who had cautiously revived and circled past Ivan, plunged in, grabbed the gun, and fired at Ivan from the floor. Ivan's revolver spat flame almost in the same instant, but the barrel of his weapon twisted upward as Gilstrom's bullet took effect. Ivan pitched forward on his face.

Delaney sprang to his feet. Ivan was a motionless heap. Gilstrom had been hit by one of Ivan's bullets. He lay on the floor, barely conscious, watching Levits stumble across the cabin. Gilstrom fired wildly and Levits reeled to one side as if someone had struck him a violent blow. He staggered toward the door, buried his head in his arms and rushed out through the flames into the freezing night.

There was a terrific gust of air. The back door had been flung open, and Delaney had a fleeting glimpse of Baldy plunging through the opening. Sam had already vanished.

Gilstrom moaned and collapsed on the floor, the gun clattering from his hand. Delaney leaped toward Gilstrom's unconscious form. Ivan, he knew, was unconscious, if not dead. Delaney grabbed Gilstrom's coat and dragged him across the floor. There was no escape by the front way now, for the whole end of the cabin was burning. He hauled and tugged at the man, knelt and got Gilstrom over his shoulders.

Delaney fought his way toward the back door and pushed Gilstrom out into the snow. He turned and ran back into the cabin, gasping for breath, the fire and smoke searing his lungs.

He found Ivan. The man was a dead weight. He hauled Ivan out into the open air. The body lay slack in the snow, arms asprawl; Ivan was through.

Levits, Baldy and Sam had taken to their heels.

The smoke was so thick Delaney could scarcely breathe. The heat seared his lungs.

Gilstrom was still unconscious, but he was breathing heavily. Blood matted the top of his head where one of Ivan's bullets had creased his skull. Delaney dashed snow into the man's face and in a few minutes Gilstrom revived. The whole cabin was ablaze now, the flames roaring through the roof and flickering wildly to the cold night sky, casting a ruddy glow upon the white slopes to the north.

Gilstrom's eyes opened.

"What—what happened?"

"Come on!" snapped Delaney, dragging the man to his feet. "We've got to get out of here."

The road that led from the town was crowded with men hurrying to the fire. In the general confusion Delaney and Gilstrom were unnoticed. They fought their way through the crowd.

No one in Portage d'Or ever knew the truth of the affair, except Levits, Sam and Baldy Kirk. No one could ever persuade them to talk of it, and they left the camp soon afterward. No one saw Dan Delaney retrieve the cache of money he had hidden in the snow, and only the man with whom he had left his dogs on the outskirts of the camp knew the details of the Snow Hawk's flight. But before the smoldering embers of Ivan's cabin had fallen into dead blackness against the snow, a sled was speeding through the night on the northern trail.

The white huskies strained at the harness as they raced on toward the shifting gray showers of the aurora that streamed in the sky. The Snow Hawk had left Portage d'Or behind, and with him was Gilstrom, the erstwhile blind man.

But the Snow Hawk's heart was heavy with a sense of defeat. He had found Ivan only to lose him again. The one man who might have given him the secret of Blackjack Adler's hiding place was dead.

Delaney had run risks and faced death—for nothing.

"I'm still under arrest, you know," Delaney reminded Gilstrom as the sled swayed and creaked over the hardpacked trail. "You're in charge. Do we go to headquarters? I'm telling you, I'll—"

Gilstrom looked at him and laughed.

"Headquarters?" he exclaimed. "Did you fall for that?"

"You're not a Mounty?" exclaimed Delaney.

Gilstrom's laughter was harsh and scornful.

"I was gunning for Ivan. That's why I came to Portage d'Or and hung around The Golden Hope. The make up fooled him, too, until he saw me without the dark glasses. Then he knew he was done for."

"You were gunning for him?" Delaney began to have a glimmer of the truth.

"He left our gang—and we don't stand for deserters. Look here," said Gilstrom, "you'd better come along with me. Things may be hot for you after what's happened back there. I'm heading back to where I belong, as fast as I can get. We have room for a guy like you. I worked that police gag because I wanted to get Ivan away from that crew and fill him full of lead without witnesses. As for you, I knew you were in a spot, and I figured we might be able to use you."

"Maybe you can," said Delaney. "What's it all about?"

"Come along, and you'll see. I'm going to a hide-out —the safest hide-out in the snow country. I'll fix it up with the chief."

"Who is your chief?"

"A guy called Blackjack Adler," said Gilstrom. "Do you want to throw in with us?"

"It's okay with me," said the Snow Hawk.

Chapter 8:
Cardigan

It was a black night and bitterly cold. In a trench scooped out of the snow two men lay huddled in their sleeping bags. A steady wind from the north sent sparks from the camp fire flickering skyward.

Somewhere out in the darkness beyond the firelight a twig snapped sharply.

Sounds carry far in freezing weather, and this noise was clear and distinct. The effect was instantaneous. One of the sleeping bags stirred into convulsive movement and a head emerged.

The Snow Hawk was as wakeful as a cat. He was up in a moment, peering out into the shadows. The firelight shone on his tense face.

He could see the scarlet embers of the blaze. He saw the motionless form of Gilstrom nearby. He, too, was a hunted man, but that faint sound from the darkness had not aroused him. Nor had there been any movement among the shadowy mounds that showed where the dogs had burrowed themselves into the snow.

The Snow Hawk groped for his gun. He thought he saw a faint movement against the pall of blackness. The silence was heavy, freighted with menace. Then it was broken. A curt voice spoke: "Put up your hands!"

The voice was hard and commanding.

The Snow Hawk's gun was out in a flash. But while his arm was still half raised he heard the crashing report of a rifle. A bullet sang past his head and kicked up a scarlet splash of embers from the fire.

Gilstrom sat up, wrenching his head and shoulders

free of the sleeping bag. He was groggy with sleep, but when he saw the Snow Hawk's upraised arms a spasm of fear contorted his face and his own hands went up.

"What the devil?" he mumbled thickly.

"We're nabbed!" said the Snow Hawk.

He ordered the dogs to be quiet. They obeyed, bristling and snarling, into the darkness.

A man emerged from the gloom and strode up into the firelight that shone upon a gleaming rifle barrel and flung a ruddy radiance upon the powerful, square-shouldered figure.

He was a Mounty—a big man, blunt-nosed, scowling, with white frost covering the stubble of beard on the lower part of his face.

"Turn out!" he ordered. "You're under arrest."

The Snow Hawk did not speak. Gilstrom licked his lips nervously and said: "I guess you've made a mistake."

"I don't make that kind of mistake. Shuck out of those sleeping bags and hand over your guns."

He meant business. The Snow Hawk and Gilstrom obeyed silently. The guns tumbled out of the eider-downs and were kicked away.

"My name," said the Mounty, "is Cardigan—Sergeant Cardigan of the Fort Remote detachment. I'm arresting *you*," he snapped, his eyes fixed steadily on the Snow Hawk, "for the shooting of Baldy Kirk and a fellow named Ivan Brodsky in Portage d'Or three days ago. More than that, you are the man who killed my friend, Sergeant Macklin, three months ago."

The Snow Hawk started. He knew now why Cardigan's voice was vibrant with hatred. And he knew that the man would welcome any false move that would justify dropping the Snow Hawk with a bullet.

"Macklin was my friend," gritted Cardigan. "I've been trailing you for a long time, Snow Hawk, and I'm glad I'm the man to take you."

"It's him you want, then," snarled Gilstrom. "You haven't anything on me. I didn't know this guy was the Snow Hawk—"

"Lay off," growled Cardigan wearily. "You were in with him on that gun play at Portage d'Or. Maybe you'll get a chance to give evidence, but you're coming along with me just the same."

Gilstrom's face was livid. He had been in and out of many prisons, and he knew what arrest meant now. It meant that he would be fingerprinted; that his record would rise up to send him back behind the bars for the rest of his days.

As for the Snow Hawk, his face did not betray his feelings. He was like a good poker player who accepts his luck, bad or otherwise, without a change of expression. His emotions, however, were not pleasant. To be trapped like this in the snow country, while still far short of his destination and far from friends, by an officer who had every reason to loathe him—it was nothing short of a disaster.

As he watched Cardigan drag a pair of jangling handcuffs from his pocket, the Snow Hawk's mind flitted swiftly over the events of the past few days. Every hour had been packed with risk and danger, and now this Mounty had overtaken him when success was almost in sight. The Snow Hawk's muscles tightened as he saw Cardigan step forward with the handcuffs.

He had braved too many risks to swallow defeat meekly at this stage of the game. A sneer flickered across his face.

"So you were Macklin's friend eh?" rasped the Snow Hawk. "What a rat he was! A no-good—"

Cardigan, face to face with the man he honestly believed to be his old friend's murderer, had been keeping his hatred under firm control. He was Macklin's avenger, it was true, but first of all he was an officer of the Mounted. Now, with this outlaw, this killer, sneering about the dead man, Cardigan's temper broke. Nothing else could have made him forget himself more completely. He lashed out at the Snow Hawk.

A blow across the mouth cut short the words. But the Snow Hawk was ready for the blow. He had played for it, invited it. His head rolled with the swinging fist. His foot went out and caught Cardigan's forearm just above the wrist in a jolting kick that sent the gun twisting loosely in the Mounty's hand.

Then the Snow Hawk was inside Cardigan's guard. One arm went across Cardigan's throat, snapping his head back. The Snow Hawk's left hand clamped on the Mounty's wrist and broke his grip on the gun.

In the very moment he struck, Cardigan realized that he had made a mistake and fallen for a trick. He fought back now, fought back with every ounce of bull strength, plunging furiously in the snow. The two men were locked in a struggle. Gilstrom, with a fierce snarl of triumph, came sidling in and leaped like a wolf at Cardigan's back.

Between them they dragged the Mounty down, overpowered him, manacled his wrists with his own handcuffs. Gilstrom, when he saw that Cardigan was helpless, plunged toward the rifle in the snow. He snatched it up, his face shining with cruel exultation in the firelight. The rifle barrel swung down.

The Snow Hawk's arm shot out. He tore the gun from Gilstrom's grasp.

"None of that!" he growled.

Gilstrom frowned. "What's the idea? You're not going to let him live, are you? We can't take him with us. If we leave him behind, he'll be on our trail again. He has to go."

"Sure! But he's my meat. If anybody is going to kill him off, I'll do the job."

The Snow Hawk prodded Cardigan with the rifle barrel. "Get up!"

The Mounty scrambled awkwardly to his feet. He stood there, head lowered like a moose at bay, his legs planted firmly apart, his hands behind his back, wrists straining at the steel links of the handcuffs.

"You're through, cop!" said the Snow Hawk coldly. He turned so that Gilstrom couldn't see his face. And he winked. "You're through, but I'm going to give you a break."

"I want no breaks from you, Snow Hawk," returned Cardigan. "Shoot and get it over with."

"You're going to get this break whether you want it or not. A quick death is better than a cop deserves. You're going to have a slow one. How long do you think you can hold out in this weather, with those handcuffs on? Half a day? A day? Maybe it'll be two days before you freeze to death."

Cardigan lowered his head. He was confident of his own ability to get back to his dogs, hidden in the bluff a quarter of a mile away. If he could get his fingers on the handcuff key—"You know I won't last until morning!" he shouted, feigning desperation.

The Snow Hawk thrust the muzzle of the gun against Cardigan's back. "Get going!"

The Mounty obeyed. He shambled off through the snow. The Snow Hawk followed and in a tense, low voice spoke to him:

"Make a break for it when I tell you. And when I shoot, drop down. It's your only chance."

The Mounty uttered an exclamation of surprise.

"Ask Maxwell about me—Dan Delaney—he'll give

you the low-down," muttered the Snow Hawk. "I've got to play with this fellow—he's got to think I knocked you off—do your stuff. Run!"

Cardigan was no fool. He had stumbled upon something he did not understand, but he realized that the Snow Hawk was not an enemy but a friend bent on saving his life.

He broke into a sudden run.

The Snow Hawk let him go no more than half a dozen paces. Then he raised the rifle and fired.

Cardigan uttered a hoarse shout, stumbled, and toppled over in the snow. He lay there without moving.

Gilstrom came running down from the camp fire.

"What the hell?" exclaimed Gilstrom, shaken. "I thought you were going to turn him loose to freeze!"

"That's what *he* thought, too," returned the Snow Hawk, with a harsh laugh. "Do you think I'd be fool enough to turn him loose—with the handcuff key in his pocket and his dogs somewhere back down the trail?"

The Snow Hawk went over to the dark form lying in the snow. He knelt for a moment and then got to his feet again. "A clean shot through the back of the head. That's the only way to deal with guys like him!"

Gilstrom looked oddly at the Snow Hawk. There was respect in his attitude now. There had been a time when Gilstrom had misgivings about his companion, when he had wondered if the Snow Hawk was really the hardened and callous criminal he was reputed to be. Those misgivings were gone. Gilstrom believed every evil thing he had ever heard of the Snow Hawk.

Chapter 9:
A Signal to Killer's Valley

They broke camp at once, hitched up the dogs, and struck out toward the north again.

"We've got to make ourselves scarce," said Gilstrom. "This is bad business. If that guy's body is found before we're safe in Killer's Valley, we'll have plenty of trouble on our hands."

And so the dark hours before dawn found them speeding on down the Bitter River. The dogs were surly and defiant, but Gilstrom showed them no mercy.

Gilstrom had been completely fooled by the Snow Hawk's ruse. He believed murder had been done, and his sole desire now was to reach that secret hiding place where "Blackjack" Adler and his fellow scoundrels took refuge from the world.

If Gilstrom had suspected the truth for a moment, the Snow Hawk's fate would have been sealed. But he thoroughly believed—as did many others in the Northland—that this reckless young dare-devil in the white parka was a callous killer, a fit recruit for the gang of criminals who acknowledged Blackjack Adler as their master.

Triumph was in sight. Within a few hours, if all went well, the Snow Hawk would learn the location of the outlaws' refuge. And then, he knew, would come the most dangerous adventure of all his colorful career in the Northland.

It was not yet dawn when Gilstrom and the Snow Hawk at last left the river and struck out to break trail up the slope near Blizzard Bluff. The place was familiar to the Snow Hawk, for it was here that he had battled his way out of one of the tightest corners of his life. The cabin on the bluff was deserted now, for Young and Keever, the whisky traders who had once occupied the place, were dead.

"Are we going to camp here?" he called out.

"No," answered Gilstrom, a dark shape against the snow ahead. "We've got to get out into the high country."

They passed the cabin, dark and sinister among the trees, and pushed on toward the snow flats to the west. A faint light was beginning to show in the sky far off in the east. Gilstrom halted and trudged back toward the sled. The dogs flung themselves into the snow.

Gilstrom came up. He peered at his companion through the gloom.

"This place we're going to," he said, "is known as Killer's Valley. No living man can reach it on foot. A mountain goat might do it, but not a man."

The Snow Hawk was puzzled. "How do we get there, then?"

"You'll see," replied Gilstrom. "The point is this—it isn't too late to turn back now."

"But I don't want to turn back."

"Listen!" said Gilstrom. "Our chief is Blackjack Adler. He is nobody's fool. There isn't one man in our gang who wouldn't swing at the end of a rope if the police got their hands on him. Understand that! Every one of us," he declared grimly, "has done murder."

"Well?"

"I warn you, if you throw in with us, you'll have to stay. When you have once set eyes on Killer's Valley, you are under our rules. If you break those rules—you die!" His voice conveyed a challenge.

The Snow Hawk did not flinch.

"I'll take my chances," he said.

He knew that his fate would be settled irrevocably by this decision. If he invaded this stronghold of desperate men, he passed sentence of death upon himself the moment his mission became known.

"Think it over," advised Gilstrom. "You can turn back now if you wish."

"You saw what happened to Cardigan," said the Snow Hawk. "Do you think I want to be picked up by the police and answer questions about that?"

Gilstrom grunted. "Okay!" he said, and began opening one of the packsacks.

The Snow Hawk watched him, still mystified. Now he knew why Gilstrom had been in Portage d'Or. Deserters from Killer's Valley did not live long to enjoy their freedom. Ivan, the deserter, was now dead.

On the way north Gilstrom had picked up the packsack from a cache beside the trail. He took from it now a number of long objects—cylinders mounted on sticks.

"Fireworks?" asked the Snow Hawk, puzzled.

Gilstrom nodded. "This," he said, thrusting the sticks deep in the snow "is how we get in touch with Killer's Valley."

He arranged the rockets to his satisfaction, then struck a match and applied it to a fuse. There was a splutter, a tiny shower of sparks, and then, with a swish and a roar, the rocket shot high into the gray gloom, splitting the darkness with crimson flame. At its zenith the rocket burst into a spreading rain of red, green, and yellow lights.

Gilstrom waited for a moment. Then he quickly applied a match to the two remaining rockets. They shot into the air within a fraction of a second of each other, trailed crimson streams of light into the sky and broke with dazzling color.

That signal, the Snow Hawk knew, could be seen for many miles by any watcher. It could be seen as far away as the Thunder Mountains, that grim and impregnable range that lay brooding in the northwest.

"You see!" remarked Gilstrom. "They will come out for us from Killer's Valley in the morning."

"But you said no man could reach the place on foot."

"That's true. But a man can reach the place with wings."

Then the Snow Hawk understood. "So!" he replied. "A plane?"

He saw now why no one had ever been able to pick up the trail of Adler's men, why no one had ever discovered that hidden refuge. Killer's Valley could be approached only from the air.

And at the same time the Snow Hawk realized that the obstacles and dangers in his path had increased tenfold.

By entering the hidden stronghold in the mountains, the Snow Hawk might well be entering a trap from which there would be no escape.

Gilstrom and Delaney made camp in the lee of a stark and rugged heap of rocks, and there beside the fire they waited patiently for the answer to their signal. It was bitterly cold that morning. Daylight came with a bleak sky, and every gust of wind that sent the snow skimming across the flats cut through their heavy garments with the stabbing thrust of a knife.

Gilstrom was nervous and watchful. His eyes were fixed on the gloomy mass of the Thunder Mountain Range, purple against the far horizon. Once in a while he got up and went around the rocks to scan the back trail toward Bitter River. It was plain that he feared pursuit.

"That cop Cardigan," he muttered, "must have been trailing us after we left Portage d'Or. How do we know he didn't have a partner with him? Those fellows usually travel in pairs. I won't feel safe until we're in the valley."

"We won't be followed," said the Snow Hawk confidently.

He wished he could have found some way of getting in touch with Jean MacLean, at the trading post on Lonely Lake, before embarking on this last and most dangerous phase of his adventure. She did not know whether he was alive or dead. It was impossible to get word to her now, for he dared not risk arousing Gilstrom's suspicions at this stage of the game.

"This guy, Sergeant Macklin," said Gilstrom—"the guy that was Cardigan's friend. Did you really knock him off?"

The Snow Hawk poked idly at the fire. Gilstrom was getting inquisitive. He looked coldly at the other man.

"Cardigan was wrong. I didn't kill Macklin."

He did not tell Gilstrom that he had promised Corporal Maxwell that he would some day solve the mystery of Macklin's death. The Mounty had been slain following the robbery of the airplane base at Fort Mishap and for a long time the Snow Hawk had been unjustly accused of this crime. He had managed to convince Corporal Maxwell of his innocence, but the mystery never had been cleared up.

Now, with the knowledge that Blackjack Adler's gang made use of a plane, he felt that there was a definite connection between that murder and the outlaw crew of Killer's Valley. It was plain to him now that the officer had died defending the supplies of gasoline and oil that the gang needed. He felt shrewdly that Gilstrom knew the true story of that affair and had merely asked the question to sound him out.

Through the clear air came a faint, throbbing sound.

The Snow Hawk gazed into the northwest, peering tensely at the gray sky above the mountain range. Then he saw a tiny speck. It grew swiftly larger, the throbbing sound became louder.

"Ah!" exclaimed Gilstrom eagerly. "They're coming out for us."

The plane swept swiftly toward them, eating up the air miles. Gilstrom sprang up, waving his arms.

The Snow Hawk's heart was pounding with excitement. This plane was at last a definite link between himself and the two prisoners he sought to rescue. He saw the big cabin machine swoop down. It circled overhead, with a crashing roar, swung far out to the east, and then slipped down in a long, easy glide, with the motor cut off.

It dropped to the surface of the open plain, its skis kicking up clouds of snow, and then the motor crashed out anew as the machine swung around and taxied toward them.

They ran out to meet it. One man descended from the plane as they approached. He stood waiting for them, thrusting back his goggles. He was a big, raw-boned fellow with a sinister scar that ran from eye to chin down one side of his evil face.

"That's Koleff!" said Gilstrom. "Adler's right-hand man."

Koleff looked capable of being the master outlaw's lieutenant. He had greenish, suspicious eyes and a mouth like a steel trap. He watched the Snow Hawk with a catlike intensity as the two men came up to him. Then his gaze rested on Gilstrom, and he rapped out one word of inquiry:

"Well?"

"A new man," Gilstrom explained. "He's okay, Koleff! If it hadn't been for him I wouldn't be here now. I got Ivan—he's dead. A Mounty caught up to us on the trail a few hours ago, and the Hawk, here, bumped him off. We've got to look after him."

Koleff grunted. "Yeah? What's your name?" he snapped.

The Snow Hawk looked at him coldly. "John Smith," he said. "But they call me the Snow Hawk."

"I've heard of you," returned Koleff. "Why do you want to throw in with us, Smith?"

"I don't want to throw in with you," replied the Snow Hawk, with a shrug, "but I'm in a hot spot if I can't find a safe hide-out mighty soon."

Koleff turned to Gilstrom. "What's the dope on this guy?" he asked.

Gilstrom told the story of the adventure in Portage d'Or, told how the Snow Hawk had helped him to escape from the gold camp, told of the affair with Cardigan. When he had finished, Koleff said to the Snow Hawk:

"You know what it means if you come in with us. You've got to stick."

"It's okay with me."

Koleff gestured toward the plane. "Get in, then."

The Snow Hawk hesitated. "How about my dogs?" he said. "That's a valuable team. I don't like to leave them like this."

"I'm coming out again in the bird today," said Koleff. "I'll see that they're looked after."

With this the Snow Hawk had to be content. It went against the grain to desert his dogs in this manner, but there was nothing else to do. He unhitched them from the sled, fed them well. They would look after themselves.

If Koleff failed to keep his promise, the dogs would eventually find their way back to the trading post at Lonely Lake or to his old cabin on Muskrat Creek, where someone would be glad enough to shelter them. The animals watched him with puzzled eyes.

Koleff took a huge red handkerchief from his pocket and came up to him as he was about to clamber into the cabin of the plane.

"You'll wear this on the way in," he said, and whipped the handkerchief across the Snow Hawk's eyes. The blindfold was swiftly knotted, and then Koleff roughly helped him into the machine.

More and more, as he sat there, he felt as if the jaws of a trap were closing about him.

Adler's men took few chances when dealing with a stranger. They did not know that the Snow Hawk was an experienced amateur aviator, that he could handle an airplane skillfully. While at university he had been one of the most enthusiastic members of the local flying club. He had hoped to get an accurate mental picture of the country while flying into Killer's Valley so that he would have directions clearly in mind should he be able to make his escape. This, now, would have to be left to chance.

He heard Koleff and Gilstrom talking quietly together. A moment later someone clambered in, he heard a brief command, then the motor spluttered and roared.

"Okay!" said Gilstrom as he crawled into the seat beside the Snow Hawk and shut the cabin door.

The engine broke into a deafening clamor. The plane lurched forward, bumped, and slipped across the snow, then gathered speed and plowed ahead until at last it took off. It droned away into the north.

Blindfolded and silent, the Snow Hawk was alone with his thoughts as the big machine hurtled swiftly through the sky toward the mysterious refuge of Killer's Valley. He was strictly on his own now, with no hope of help from the outside world. He had delivered himself into the hands of unscrupulous enemies who would not hesitate to riddle him with bullets at the slightest hint of his real purpose.

Chapter 10:
A Dangerous Reunion

The Snow Hawk experienced a sensation of utter helplessness during that strange journey. He could see nothing; he heard nothing but the deafening roar of the plane. He knew in a vague way that the machine was carrying him toward the Thunder Mountains, but to what part of that great and desolate range he did not know and could not guess.

As nearly as he could estimate, it was twenty minutes before the flight came to an end. There was a slow series of spirals, a steep, swift glide ending with a sudden shock and a series of bumps and lurches as the plane straightened out and taxied through the snow.

Delaney sat motionless as the engine was shut off. The roar died abruptly, but his ears still rang with the throbbing clamor. He heard Gilstrom say:

"We're here!"

A hand tugged at the knot of the handkerchief, and the blindfold was whisked away. He blinked and looked around. He saw the hard faces of his companions, saw white snow through the cabin window. Then Gilstrom opened the door and clambered out.

"Come on!"

Delaney followed. And then, standing in the snow beside Gilstrom, he had his first glimpse of Killer's Valley.

It was an immense, natural bowl in the heart of the mountains. The snow-covered floor was a level plain, and the sides sloped gradually at first in wooded inclines, then rose sharply to steep, rocky cliffs and finally to the harsh and tremendous barricades of the peaks.

It was a wild and terrible place, like some gigantic

crater of the moon. A few hundred yards away, huddled in the shelter of a great sheer wall of rock, he saw a group of log cabins with smoke curling from the chimneys; but in all the desolate valley this was the only sign of human life. The cabins were dwarfed by the great mountains that towered to the bleak sky in jagged pinnacles as far as the eye could see in every direction.

This was Killer's Valley, the retreat of hunted men. Delaney felt a grudging admiration for Blackjack Adler, who had chosen this refuge. A more impregnable sanctuary for murderers could not be imagined. The Thunder Mountain Range, as Delaney knew, had never been explored. This valley was marked on no maps. It was cut off from the world by the leagues of frozen wilderness that lay beyond the mountain walls. And apparently there was but one way of access or escape—by air.

He looked around to see Koleff grinning at him, the scar standing out white and livid against the man's cheek.

"Even at that," said Koleff, "it's better than the penitentiary."

"Or the rope," muttered Gilstrom.

Delaney gazed up at the snowstreaked mountains that walled in the valley, at the tall trees that rose in successive ranks from the grim slopes. No human being could scale those terrible heights.

It struck him then that the men of Killer's Valley had merely exchanged one prison for another. His alert eyes took in every detail of the stronghold, seeking vainly for an outlet. He saw none.

"Come on," said Koleff. "We'll go up and see the chief."

They trudged through the snow toward the cluster of cabins at the foot of the cliff. Delaney could see dark figures moving about the buildings. One man came down the path, talked briefly with Koleff for a moment, and then went on toward the plane to check it over.

"We'll bring you to Adler first," said Gilstrom. "Don't lie to him. But don't be too soft, either. He likes men with nerve."

They approached the largest of all the cabins. A group of half a dozen men standing nearby looked at Delaney curiously. Koleff and Gilstrom exchanged greetings with them.

The door of the big cabin opened as they drew near, and an old man emerged, carrying a broom and a basket of rubbish. His shoulders were bent, and he shuffled wearily.

Dan Delaney's heart skipped a beat. His hands clenched quickly as he fought to keep control of himself.

The old man was his father!

Matt Delaney looked tired and dispirited. His long imprisonment in the mountain retreat had evidently taken toll of his vitality. He stepped aside as the three men came up to the doorway.

Dan could scarcely restrain the impulse to rush toward him and make himself known, but he knew that would be fatal. The situation was dangerous enough as it was.

Somehow, it had not occurred to him that his father would be allowed to move about at will; he had pictured Matt Delaney held under lock and key. But here was his father almost face to face with him.

He turned his head aside, trying to evade recognition. And then:

"Dan!"

Delaney wheeled, frowning. His father was staring at him. The broom had dropped from Matt Delaney's nerveless hand.

Koleff looked around swiftly, his eyes alert with suspicion. Gilstrom's mouth fell open in surprise.

"Dan!" exclaimed the old man. "Have they caught you, too?"

Delaney looked at Koleff, then at Gilstrom, desperately trying to feign bewilderment.

"Who is the old bird talking to?" he demanded.

"You!" snapped Koleff dangerously. "Do you know him?" He wheeled on Matt Delaney. "What's the idea? You know this fellow?"

"I never saw him in my life," growled Delaney. "What's it all about?"

Matt Delaney realized that he had blundered. His natural assumption had been that his son was being brought to the cabin as a prisoner. He leaned forward, peering closely at Dan. Then he shook his head.

"I—I'm sorry," he muttered. "I made a mistake. I thought he was a man I knew."

Koleff was not so easily satisfied. "Mistake?" he snarled. "You're sure?"

"I guess my eyes aren't as good as they used to be," said Matt Delaney. "No—I don't know this fellow. At first, I thought—but it isn't the same man." He turned away, shaking his head and muttering to himself.

Delaney felt sick with suspense. If his father had not succeeded in covering up the blunder, his mission to Killer's Valley would be ended before it really began. But Koleff seemed satisfied.

Gilstrom said: "The old boy is weak in the head. Forget it."

He knocked at the cabin door. A deep voice bade them enter.

After the harsh, white light of the snow-covered valley the cabin seemed very dark, although a blazing fire roared and crackled in a huge stone fireplace. Delaney, as he stepped across the threshold, had an impression of a long, gloomy room with fur rugs on the floors and pelts of bear and caribou on the walls. But the details were of little account.

The room was dominated by a man; and that man, he instantly knew, was Blackjack Adler.

Blackjack Adler sat at a heavy, homemade table, slouching in a great armchair carved out of pine. Before him stood a young man, pale, unkempt, and ragged.

Blackjack Adler was an old man with a white, patriarchal beard that covered his chest. He was as bald as an eagle, with a visage of the same sinister cruelty. Under beetling white brows his eyes glittered like black ice. His heavy, blue-veined hands were clenched on the table before him.

Blackjack Adler was old, but his shoulders were still massive; his thickset body gave an impression of indomitable strength. He looked like a wise and venerable prophet, with the difference that his wisdom was the wisdom of evil.

Adler darted a swift, penetrating glance at them, then waved one hand in an impatient gesture. He turned again to the young man who stood before him. "You're still stubborn, then?" he said in a rasping voice.

The young man, slender, well built, with long, uncombed hair and a heavy growth of unshaven beard, said evenly:

"Shove it!"

"All right, MacLean!" growled the outlaw. "You won't be so stubborn before I'm through with you. This is your last chance. You and the old man found gold on Carcajou Creek. You won't tell me where to find that strike. But I mean to have it!"

"I'm not talking."

"You'll talk when your sister is brought to Killer's Valley!" roared Adler.

MacLean's fists clenched. "That's a bluff."

"I never bluff," said Adler. "If you want to save your sister, you had better talk now."

Delaney was rigid, his face expressionless, feigning indifference to the scene. He knew that the young man was Douglas MacLean, his father's partner, brother of Jean MacLean, and that this was the crisis of Adler's long effort to force from his prisoners the secret of the gold find. Adler was trying to break down MacLean's resistance by threatening harm to Jean.

"I'm not telling you about the gold find," snapped MacLean, "because I know what it will mean. As soon as you have the information, Matt and I will be shot. I'm not a fool."

"When your pretty sister is brought into Killer's Valley," rumbled Adler, "you'll sing a different tune. Get out!"

MacLean shrugged and went over to the door. When he had gone, Adler turned in his chair.

"Tell your story, Gilstrom!" he ordered. "Did you kill Ivan? Who is this new man? Why is he here? Where did you find him?"

Delaney felt that those icy old eyes were boring directly through him, hunting for the slightest evidence of treachery. Blackjack Adler had been a scoundrel and a captain of scoundrels for more than half a century in the wildest parts of the world. Delaney had a feeling that every thought in his head could be read unerringly by those eyes.

Gilstrom was speaking. He told how he had tracked Ivan, the deserter, to Portage d'Or, how he had disguised himself as a blind man the better to watch Ivan's movements in the gold camp, how he had come in touch with the Snow Hawk, and how they had fled from the camp after their desperate battle with Ivan and Baldy Kirk. He told of their capture by Cardigan and of their escape.

"The Snow Hawk killed that Mounty," said Gilstrom. "He's wanted on a couple of other raps besides, so I brought him in with me."

Blackjack Adler looked at Delaney for a long time. When he spoke his voice was deceptively mild.

"I have heard of you," he said. "What is your real name?"

Delaney grinned scornfully. "Smith," he said.

"Dan?" asked Koleff. Old Matt Delaney's exclamation outside the cabin still stuck in his memory.

"John," returned Delaney. "And that's as near my real name as you'll ever get."

Adler stroked his white beard. "Cardigan arrested you for shooting this other Mounty—Macklin. Did you kill Macklin?"

Delaney shook his head. He recognized this for a trap. "Cardigan was wrong that time. One of your men did that job, wearing a white parka like mine."

Blackjack Adler nodded and looked at Gilstrom. "Cardigan was very close to the right man, if he had only known it."

Delaney knew then that the murderer of Sergeant Macklin was Gilstrom.

Chapter 11:
Secret Mission

Delaney was not admitted to the gang until he had undergone a shrewd cross-examination. Blackjack Adler questioned him closely, and had the Snow Hawk been less alert he would have been tripped up. He held closely, however, to his pose as an outlaw fleeing from the police, and at last it was evident that his inquisitor was satisfied.

"You have a gun?" said Adler.

"Yes."

"Hand it over."

Delaney put his revolver on the table.

"In Killer's Valley," said Adler, "I am the only man who goes armed. If there are disputes, I settle them."

Delaney shrugged with a pretense of indifference. It was a blow, nevertheless, to learn that he was to be unarmed.

"I am seventy years old," growled Blackjack Adler. "I have lived this long because I trust no man. I don't trust any human being alive." He gestured toward the door. "Go out and tell the old man he is to bring your packsack up from the plane and show you where you are to sleep. Koleff, I want to talk to you and Gilstrom."

The others hitched their chairs closer to the table. Delaney went outside.

When he closed the door behind him he breathed deeply of the crisp, cold air. In his wildest imaginings he had never believed that such apparently insurmountable obstacles would confront him when he at last discovered his father. How he was going to rescue him, he did not know; it seemed impossible that he could even escape from Killer's Valley himself.

He saw Matt Delaney trudging up the slope with a packsack on his back. The old man had already been down to the plane for Dan's belongings. Each was careful to give no sign of recognition. They knew that watchful eyes might be upon them.

"Where am I to stay?" asked Delaney roughly.

"If you'll come with me, I'll show you," muttered the old man. He went on up the path toward the row of cabins.

Delaney was quartered in a crude but sturdy log cabin which he shared with three others.

"Sailor" Skene, a brutal, bull-necked ruffian with one ear and a battle-scarred face, had served for years on Adler's pirate craft in the arctic seas and the northern Pacific.

Beniah Brown was a fat, gross man who had escaped from an American penitentiary three days before the date set for his execution, knifing two guards in his break for liberty.

Max Krug was a bullet-headed rogue with a pock-marked face, an international scoundrel who was wanted by the police of five nations.

The three men welcomed Delaney indifferently and asked him no questions. But they were sizing him up. They sat slouching on the sides of their bunks and watched him.

"The Snow Hawk, eh?" said Sailor Skene. "They made it too hot for you."

"That's right." Delaney grinned.

"You are not so smart as you thought, hey?" said Krug.

"No, I'm not so smart."

Matt Delaney came back into the cabin with an armload of firewood. It galled Delaney, wrenched his heart, to see the old man performing these menial tasks, but he hid his feelings. It was just another score against Blackjack Adler, and there would be a time of reckoning. Soon!

Matt Delaney trudged over to the stove. Beniah Brown, with a sly grin, stuck out his foot. The old man tripped over it and fell sprawling. The heavy birch sticks crashed against Sailor Skene's legs.

The Sailor stormed to his feet with an oath. He swooped, dragged Matt Delaney to his feet. A heavy fist smashed viciously against the old man's face. He crumpled to the floor with a moan.

Dan Delaney had told himself that he must keep himself under control, that he must avoid the faintest show of interest in Adler's prisoners; but flesh and blood revolted against this.

He was across the cabin at a stride, his eyes alight with a cold fire of rage. His right fist whipped out and cracked against Sailor Skene's jaw.

The Sailor went back, but he didn't go down. Roaring with surprise and fury, he straightened up and then stormed in with swinging fists. He was the slugger type, hero of a hundred rough-and-tumble battles on shipboard, and his big clenched paws swung like clubs.

Delaney ducked, dodged, smashed two driving blows to Skene's face, and then slipped back out of range. Krug and Beniah Brown were on their feet, yelping, but they did not interfere.

Sailor Skene rushed, heavy feet thudding on the floor, and this time one of those sledge-hammer fists caught Delaney on the side of the head.

It was a stunning blow; it almost paralyzed him. He covered up and weathered a brutal flurry of savage punches until his head cleared. Then he pounded Skene's ribs, drawing gasps of pain from the big fellow.

Skene clinched, but Delaney fought his way free and backed across the cabin. Skene was after him. They circled the stove, Krug and Beniah Brown scrambled wildly to get out of the way. Delaney saw his father crawling painfully to his feet. The door was flung open. Men were crowding across the threshold.

Skene rushed. A terrific smash to the face rocked Delaney. He stumbled and went down on one knee. A slashing kick from Skene's heavy boot would have put him out of business if he hadn't seen it coming. He rolled to one side, and Skene staggered off-balance as the kick missed.

Delaney came up, groggy, and put all his strength into a left that came from his knees and blasted against the Sailor's chin. Then they were at it again, hammer and tongs, panting, slugging, surging from wall to wall. The battle had drawn every man in the camp to the doorway. Delaney was tiring. It seemed impossible to break down Skene's iron strength. Skene rushed him again. Delaney weaved, dodged, boxed cautiously, waited for an opening.

It came. Delaney's fist seemed to travel no more than a few inches, but when it cracked against his opponent's jaw Skene's head shot back. A glassy look came into his eyes. He lashed out mechanically, and the blow struck Delaney's head, but there was no force behind it. Delaney slammed over the right.

Skene's arms dropped, his body sagged, he swayed drunkenly on his heels. Delaney doubled him up with a crushing jolt to the stomach. The Sailor was out on his feet. Delaney measured him and drove a straight left to the jaw.

Sailor Skene crashed to the floor and lay there, twitching.

"You've licked the Sailor!" exclaimed Krug in awe.

Delaney looked around at the crowd of men in the doorway. In the forefront stood Blackjack Adler. The master outlaw was thoughtfully stroking his beard.

"So!" muttered Adler. He regarded Delaney with

new interest. It was, to Adler's knowledge, the first time Sailor Skene had ever been whipped. "How did this start?"

"The Sailor knocked the old fellow down," explained Krug, gesturing toward Matt Delaney.

"And our new man didn't like it?" inquired Adler softly.

Krug nodded.

"So!" remarked Adler again, more thoughtful than ever. There was something ominous and brooding in his attitude. Then he shrugged. The men stood aside to let him pass.

After a while Sailor Skene got slowly to his feet. He looked at Delaney, his face sullen, his eyes full of hatred.

"I'll even this score," he growled and lurched outside.

Delaney knew he had made an enemy.

Some of the outlaws remained in the cabin. They made it plain that they were not yet prepared to accept the Snow Hawk as one of them, but it was also obvious that he had won their respect.

"Watch your step," advised Beniah Brown. "The Sailor won't forget this in a hurry. He has killed men for less than what you did to him."

Delaney laughed scornfully. "He has no gun."

"No," said Brown, "but there are knives."

There was something about Blackjack Adler's attitude that disturbed him. The old outlaw was shrewd. Was he shrewd enough to draw his own conclusions from old Matt Delaney's involuntary recognition of the Snow Hawk as linked up with Delaney's fight with Sailor Skene?

He would have to act, and act quickly. Every hour he remained in this valley increased his danger. The airplane was his one hope. Possession of the plane must be his trump card in any effort at rescue of the prisoners, but in the first place he must get in touch with his father and young MacLean. There must be some concerted plan, and it must succeed at the first attempt.

In the distance he heard a dull, spluttering roar. He sat up sharply. It was the motor of the plane. The roar settled down to a steady throbbing.

"There's something in the wind," said Beniah Brown, looking up. "Koleff and Gilstrom are taking off again."

Delaney got up and went over to the door. He opened it and looked out.

The plane was moving slowly across the snow down on the valley floor. The roar became louder, the plane moved faster, its skis half hidden.

Delaney stood in the doorway as if stunned. With a sinking heart he saw the big machine skimming across the snow. It rose from the surface, climbed into the air, banked, circled, and rose higher. It came roaring above the cabins and moved upward in a steadily widening spiral. Then it straightened out and went throbbing out of sight above the mountain barrier.

Adler had decided to waste no further time. Jean MacLean was to be brought to Killer's Valley in order to force the prisoners to terms.

Delaney went back to his bunk. The trump card, for the time being, had been snatched out of his reach. And if Koleff and Gilstrom succeeded in abducting Jean, the situation would be even more complicated.

There were twelve men in this outlaw colony—Adler, Koleff, Gilstrom, Skene, Krug, and seven assorted ruffians exclusive of Matt Delaney, Doug McLean, and himself. There was no way, so far as he could see, of getting in touch with the prisoners without risking disaster to the whole enterprise. He would have to play a lone hand.

Chapter 12:
Abduction

Cardigan of the Mounted was in the trading post at Lonely Lake that afternoon telling Jean MacLean the story of his strange adventure the previous night.

"So then, when he might have drilled me, the fellow fired into the air. I tumbled over and played dead."

Jean's eyes were shining. Cardigan's visit had brought her the first news of the Snow Hawk in days. "It must have been because of the man who was with him," she said. "He was playing a part. Who was he?"

"A fellow named Gilstrom. They both had been in Portage d'Or. But do you mean to tell me, Jean, that I've been wrong all this time? The Snow Hawk didn't kill Macklin? He's one of us himself?"

Jean nodded. "I have told you the story. The Snow Hawk is as straight as any man in the Mounted—"

She was interrupted by the frenzied howling of the dogs outside. Jean ran to the window. Down the trail swung a team of matched white huskies. On the sled crouched a dark-clad man, but gripping the handles at the rear was a tall figure in white parka and hood. Jean uttered a cry. "It's the Snow Hawk," she exclaimed.

The white Huskies, the white fur garments, were all familiar to her. She flew to the door. Then, with her hand already on the knob, she turned.

"You had better stay out of sight!" she exclaimed breathlessly. "That man Gilstrom is with him. If Gilstrom believes you are dead—"

Cardigan realized the common sense of this proposal. It might spoil the Snow Hawk's game, whatever it was, if he appeared on the scene now.

Jean ran down the snow trail to meet the oncoming team. Eagerly she cried out: 'I'm glad you're back!"

Not until the sled swung quickly up to her, however, did she realize her mistake. These were the Snow Hawk's dogs, this was the Snow Hawk's famous white parka, but those were not the Snow Hawk's eyes. A great white arm swept out; she was hauled swiftly down toward the sled.

Jean, taken utterly off her guard, shrieked: "Cardigan!" And then her cries were muffled by the heavy furs that were flung over her head. She was helpless in the grip of the man on the sled. The white-clad driver lashed the Huskies, swung them around on the trail.

Cardigan came lunging out onto the porch. He had heard that call for help. He saw the team racing away from the post, saw the struggling figures on the sled, saw the man in the white parka flailing the dogs with the whip. His gun barked. He ran down the trail. The man in the white parka turned and fired.

Cardigan drilled another bullet at the swaying figure, and the man pitched backward into the snow. The dogs came to a stop. The dark-clad figure leaped from the sled and hauled the body up onto the sled. Jean was struggling to free herself from the furs.

Cardigan came running down the trail. The dark-clad man whirled and fired. Cardigan dropped with a shattered knee. The dogs were fleeing northward. "It was the Snow Hawk!" groaned Cardigan. Then he collapsed, half fainting from the pain of his bullet-smashed knee.

Chapter 13:
The Knife

It was twilight in Killer's Valley when Delaney heard the distant humming of the plane.

All afternoon he had endured the suspense of waiting; all afternoon he had watched for an opportunity to have a word with either his father or young MacLean. He had been blocked at every turn. One of Adler's men seemed to be constantly at his elbow.

Delaney had an idea that this was not by accident. He felt that Blackjack Adler was suspicious and that orders had been given that he was to be watched. He saw the two prisoners often that afternoon, but by neither word nor sign did he give away any indication that he was interested in them.

He was in the cabin when the throbbing hum of the plane sounded above the mountain ring. Delaney looked up. Sailor Skene, who had been watching him sullenly from across the room, strode toward the door. Krug, a bulky shadow on his bunk in the gloom, got up and followed.

The roar of the plane grew louder. Against the patch of sky visible through the window Delaney saw the machine swinging over the range. Sailor Skene and Krug went outside and down the path. Delaney stood on the threshold and watched the plane circling as it gradually descended.

Most of the men were emerging from their cabins, moving down to the valley floor where the plane would land. Delaney did not see his father or young MacLean. He remained where he was, his eyes fixed on the plane as it came swooping down in the twilight.

Then he heard a voice: "Dan!"

It was his father's voice. He saw a shadowy figure at the corner of the cabin.

"Yes."

"Why did you come here? It's foolish. We can't get away, son. Adler has all the guns. It's no use, Dan. You had better try to get outside again."

"And leave you here, dad? Nothing doing. But it will have to be tonight. Can you get in touch with young MacLean and tell him to be ready?"

"But what's your plan?" asked the old man hoarsely. "You can't take off in the plane after dark. We'll never make it. We'll be shot down."

"We've got to try it," insisted Delaney. "And we must be armed. Where does Adler keep the guns?"

"In his cabin, under lock and key. But here—I have this."

The old man advanced cautiously around the corner of the cabin. In the dim light they could scarcely be seen by the outlaws down by the plane. The big machine was just coming to a stop on the white field of snow. An object was slipped into Delaney's hand, and then his father slipped away again.

The object was an ordinary table knife, but the blade had been sharpened to a keen edge. Delaney slipped the weapon into his pocket—for it was as a weapon he meant to use it if he failed to get possession of a gun.

His father had vanished around the corner of the cabin.

"Dad!" said Delaney softly. "Are you there?"

But there was no answer.

Delaney heard crunching footsteps in the snow. He whirled around and, with a shock, saw the bulky figure of Blackjack Adler not ten feet away. The old pirate had emerged from his own cabin and had come down the path in the dim light so quietly that Delaney was taken completely by surprise.

"You were talking to someone?" grated Adler.

Even in the gloom his fierce old eyes seemed to flash with a dangerous fire.

Delaney was cool. "To myself, probably," he said. "It's a habit I have."

Adler faced him, feet wide apart, hands thrust into the side pockets of his coat, head thrust forward.

"Do you think you are going to like it here, Mr.——Snow Hawk?" he asked suddenly.

"It is much, much better than the penitentiary."

Adler looked down at the crowd of men about the great winged shape of the plane, black against the snow.

"I think," he said, "that we have a visitor."

Some of the men had left the plane and were coming up across the flats. Delaney could see that two men were clinging to a struggling figure, dragging their prisoner through the snow.

His mouth tightened. Had they actually captured Jean? Then he heard Adler chuckle.

"A lady!" said Adler, and went on down the path.

Jean, then, had been abducted.

Somehow, Delaney had never thought that Gilstrom and Koleff would be able to accomplish their mission. Jean was a self-reliant, courageous girl, well able to take care of herself.

Delaney frowned as he realized how this new development complicated the affair. There were three to rescue now, and Jean's arrival here meant that the break for liberty must take place at once. Blackjack Adler would lose no time in playing this trump card, in forcing his prisoners to reveal the secret of the gold in order to save Jean from harm.

The men were coming up the trail now. Delaney

went back into the cabin. He did not want to take any chance on Jean's recognition of him. He sat beside the glowing stove and sought a plan of action. Outside he heard the dull murmur of voices, the shuffling of feet in the snow. In the distance a door slammed.

A man came into the cabin. A match flared, and the man lighted a lamp. The yellow glow revealed Sailor Skene. The light shone on his blunt, brutal features. He held the lamp on high, looked down at Delaney.

"You're wanted!" he growled.

"Who wants me?"

"Adler. You're to come into the big cabin."

"What's it all about?"

"Don't ask questions," snarled the Sailor.

Delaney got up. He was uneasy, but there was nothing he could do. He had to obey this summons. He walked out, scarcely glancing at Skene. The Sailor followed him.

The big cabin was illuminated by flickering lamps. When Delaney stepped across the threshold he was conscious of the sullen glances of the outlaws, all of whom were crowded in the cabin. His searching gaze found Jean. She was sitting beside Adler's table, the lamplight shining on her white, tense face. If she was frightened, her features did not reveal the fact.

Adler, like a spider in his web, was sitting behind the table. He watched Jean's face as Delaney came in. But she betrayed no recognition. A startled light flashed into her eyes for a mere fraction of a second, but that was all. Behind Adler stood Koleff, his face grim, the scar on his face standing out livid and ugly in the light.

Sailor Skene closed the door and then stood behind Delaney with folded arms.

Adler's eyes bored through Delaney. He seemed to be savoring this moment. Then he said: "Snow Hawk —it's all up with you."

Delaney was cool. Something had happened. Adler had learned the truth. How, he did not know. But he was trapped.

His eyes rested on a revolver that lay within reach of Blackjack Adler's hand. He estimated the distance between himself and the table.

"What do you mean?" he asked coolly.

"Gilstrom is dead!"

Delaney shrugged. "What has that to do with me?"

"You sent him to his death, damn you!" shouted Koleff, his face twisting with fury. "That Mounty—"

"Quiet!" thundered Adler. "I'll handle this." His eyes settled on Delaney again. "I suspected you," he growled, "from the beginning. And now I know. I suspected you when the old man recognized you and called you by name. I suspected you when you attacked Sailor Skene because of the old man. I suspected you when I found you talking to the old man a few minutes ago. And now Koleff brings news. You tricked Gilstrom. You didn't shoot that Mounty. And how do I know? Because Cardigan was the Mounty who shot Gilstrom this afternoon. You didn't kill Cardigan. You let him escape. And what does it mean? It means that you are a spy!"

The outlaws were muttering.

"A spy!" shouted Delaney, stepping forward angrily. "Gilstrom himself told you how we got out of Portage d'Or only by the skin of our teeth." He was within three paces of the gun now, playing for time. "What proof have you that Cardigan is alive?" He advanced another step. "Do you think Gilstrom would be such a fool as to bring me in here if he wasn't sure of me? I didn't ask to come—"

And then, suddenly, Delaney lunged toward the revolver.

Chapter 14:
A Deal

Sailor Skene had been watching the Snow Hawk like a lynx. At that, Delaney's bid for the gun had been so sudden and so well-timed that he nearly succeeded. His hand was just closing on the butt of the weapon when Skene, with a roar of fury, was upon him.

Delaney was hurled violently to one side. Skene's hand closed on his wrist. Skene's left arm hooked savagely around his neck. Delaney flung himself around and tried to hold his grip on the gun, but within the next moment half a dozen of the outlaws had flung themselves upon him. He was borne to the floor, struggling.

Blackjack Adler scarcely moved in his chair. He watched impassively, with a grim smile.

Delaney was dragged to his feet, with Skene and Koleff clinging to his arms. Blackjack Adler got up. He walked around the table.

"So!" gritted the master outlaw. "A spy, eh?"

His arm swung. His fist smashed directly into Delaney's face. Blackjack Adler had lost little of his brute strength, even at seventy.

Jean MacLean uttered a cry of anger. Adler turned on her.

"You have only begun to see how we treat spies in Killer's Valley," he said, and went back behind the table.

One of the outlaws found a length of rope. Koleff and Sailor Skene bound Delaney's arms tightly. Adler gave a curt order to two of the other men, and they vanished from the cabin.

Delaney was silent. He had made his bid for freedom, and he had lost.

The door opened. The two outlaws returned, with old Matt Delaney and young MacLean.

Jean sprang to her feet at the sight of her brother.

"Doug!" she cried, and before anyone could stop her she ran to him and buried her face against his shoulder.

Doug MacLean said nothing, but over Jean's head he darted a look of hatred at Blackjack Adler. Until now he had been proud and defiant; but now, at the sight of his sister in Adler's power, his resistance seemed broken.

"You white-bearded old devil!" he gritted at last. And then his shoulders slumped. His hand stroked the head of the sobbing girl.

Blackjack Adler, however, paid scant attention to this scene. He was looking at old Matt Delaney, scrutinizing the veteran prospector's weather-beaten features. Then he nodded.

"I thought so," he said to the Snow Hawk. "I thought so. Father and son."

"Aye!" said Matt Delaney. "And now it's a bargain you want to make, I suppose."

Blackjack Adler pounded the table suddenly with hiis fist. "Bargain be damned!" he declared harshly. "You'll do as I say. You see your son there. I can have him shot before your eyes. I can do it myself," he said, snatching up the revolver. "I've killed men in my time! I would think no more of it than killing a fly."

He flung out one arm, pointing at Doug MacLean. "As for you!" he roared. "Are you so high and mighty now? Would you like your sister to stay here in Killer's Valley? With my men?" he said. "With me!"

MacLean flushed with anger. He strode forward, fists clenched. Sailor Skene lunged menacingly. Jean grasped his arm.

"Doug!" she whispered. "Please!"

"You see what I can do!" thundered Adler. "You know what I want. I want that gold find, and I mean to have it."

Matt Delaney stepped forward. The lamplight shone on his gray hair, his worn features. "Let us go," he said, "and you can have the gold."

"Draw me a map!" demanded Adler eagerly. He snatched up a pen and a sheet of paper, thrust them across the table. "Draw me a map of the place."

"And you'll let us go?"

"I give you my word!" shouted Adler. "I give you my word on it. But I'm to have that gold. No tricks. No interference. You'll swear on the Bible that you'll tell no one of this valley; that you'll say nothing to anyone of what has happened here."

Matt Delaney's thin, trembling hand crept toward the pen.

"Dad!" said the Snow Hawk sharply. "Don't let him have that map. You can't trust him."

Adler got up from his chair. He handed the revolver to Sailor Skene. He gestured toward the Snow Hawk.

"Sailor!" he ordered. "Take this fellow outside. Put a bullet through him."

Skene grabbed the revolver, his eyes gleaming with eagerness.

Doug MacLean said hoarsely: "Let him have the map. Let him have it, Matt."

Matt Delaney had already picked up the pen. Skene seized Delaney by the shoulder and swung him around.

Adler spoke: "All right, Sailor. They're listening to reason now."

Skene's disappointment was plain. He cursed and tossed the gun back onto the table.

Delaney knew very well that by giving Adler the map his father was sacrificing the last possible chance of safety. The man's word was worthless. Even if he knew the secret of the gold, Adler could never hope to get possession of it if even one of his prisoners got to the authorities with the facts.

There was, however, no way out. The old pirate held the whip hand. He could play one prisoner against the other. Doug MacLean, anxious for the safety of Jean; and Matt Delaney, anxious to save the life of his son. But the Snow Hawk knew that their fate was sealed when Adler once knew the secret of the gold.

The old man was drawing his map. Blackjack Adler leaned across the table, watching closely.

"Here," muttered Matt Delaney, "is Carcajou Creek. And here is where we were camped when you and your men took us away."

"But you weren't camped near your gold find," said Adler. "We went over every inch of the ground for miles."

Matt Delaney shook his white head.

"No; we were on our way out then. We made our strike away back here"—and he marked a place on the map—"back near the headwaters of the creek. It's in the hill country."

As he went on, carefully describing landmarks and indicating distances on the crudely scrawled map, the outlaws moved closer to the table. There is a fascination in the very thought of gold. The map attracted them like a magnet. Even Sailor Skene moved from Delaney's side, peering at the sheet of paper in the lamplight.

"It is rich?" said Blackjack Adler.

"I've prospected for years," said Matt Delaney. "You saw the samples we had with us. I've never seen a bigger showing of free gold in my life." He tossed down the pen. "Much good it will do you," he said bitterly. "You'll never be able to work it."

"I have my own plans about that," said Adler. "I

won't work it. I'll sell it. When there's a million-dollar gold mine in sight, a man can do plenty. Cash down, an interest in the mine, and no questions asked. There's a man in Edmonton can put it through for me."

He looked around at the hard, swarthy faces of his men. "Boys," he declared exultantly, "we'll live the good life in South America for the rest of our years. With a gold mine behind us we don't need to be afraid of any law that was ever made."

Delaney, listening to this, knew that Blackjack Adler's scheme had one great flaw, and that flaw was the existence of the prisoners. He knew how Adler would deal with that. There was no hope for them.

Delaney had been unobtrusively working at the ropes that bound his arms. He could not free himself, but he had managed to work his right hand around until it was close to his pocket. And in his pocket was the sharpened table knife his father had given him.

"Now," Matt Delaney was saying, "I have given you the map. You have given us your word that you'll set us free."

Blackjack Adler's eyes were contemptuous. "Am I a fool?" he rasped. "A fake map; I set you free—and what happens?"

"The map is no fake," declared the old man steadily.

"But how can I tell? No, sir! You don't leave this valley until I have found that gold and until the deal is put through."

"But that will take months!" cried Jean hotly. "You gave your word."

"My word—bah!" scoffed Adler. "If I always kept my word, I wouldn't be alive today."

"I knew it!" shouted Doug MacLean angrily.

Adler rose. He gestured to Koleff and one of the other men.

"Take them out of here!" he roared. "Take them

away and lock them up. But leave the girl—and the spy."

Matt Delaney had courage. When he realized that his sacrifice had been for nothing he crouched, his old eyes blazing. Then he sprang at Adler. But Koleff intervened at a bound and flung the old man roughly back against the wall.

Doug MacLean was struggling like a maniac as Beniah Brown and Krug dragged him away from Jean. For a moment the cabin was a confusion of shifting figures. The flurry lasted only a few seconds. Matt and young MacLean were hustled out of the cabin.

The Snow Hawk had not been idle during the excitement. No one saw the quick wrench of his arm as he worked his hand at last to the very top of his pocket. His groping fingers felt the reassuring blade. But he made no attempt to use it just then. That knife was his one slim hope, and he could afford to take no chances of a blunder that might result in its discovery.

He was bound, it was true, but a knife can cut rope, and he held a certain advantage in the fact that he was believed to be unarmed. When the door slammed behind the struggling figures he slipped his arm back beneath the loosened ropes. To all outward indications he was as tightly bound as ever.

Half a dozen outlaws remained in the cabin, including Skene. Blackjack Adler waved them away, with the exception of the Sailor.

"Get out!" he ordered curtly.

With sullen faces they shambled out of the cabin.

"A spy," said Adler heavily, "deserves no mercy. And from me he gets none. What have you to say for yourself, Snow Hawk?"

"Nothing."

"You knew the risks you were running?"

"I knew," replied Delaney. "I lost. Get it over with."

"It will be over soon enough," Adler assured him.

"For all that you have given the others your word, they have no more chance of escaping from this valley alive than I have."

"That's true enough," growled Adler. "I'd be a fool to let them go free to ruin my plans. No, it's to be a clean sweep. As soon as I satisfy myself that the old man did not lie to me and that the gold is really where he says it is—well—they'll die, too."

"And the girl?"

Adler looked at Jean. His dull eyes roved over her flushed face.

"Perhaps," he said, "after a few months in Killer's Valley, she may be glad to come to South America with us."

"I'll kill myself first!" declared Jean.

"You will not be given the chance," said Adler.

He turned to Skene. "All right, Sailor. You'd like to get even for the beating you got today?" He shoved the revolver across the table. "There are six bullets in the gun. Perhaps you'd like to make him dance a bit. Perhaps you'd like to finish him with the first bullet. But not here, Sailor. Not here. Outside. Outside in the snow." He gestured toward the door.

Jean was wild with terror. She ran to Delaney and flung her arms around him. "They can't do this!" she cried. "They can't. It's murder."

Sailor Skene, with a growl, tore her arms from around Delaney's neck and thrust the girl back into her chair. Blackjack Adler uttered a roar of delight.

"So!" he mocked. "Lovers, eh? Well, then, she'll need comforting. Go ahead, Sailor. Take him away."

Sailor Skene jammed the barrel of the gun into Delaney's ribs. "Get going!" he snarled. "We are going for a little walk. Only you're not coming back."

Chapter 15:
Desperate Measures

It was pitch dark outside when the Snow Hawk stepped across the threshold of the cabin, with Sailor Skene close behind him. A beam of yellow light fell across the white snow, and then it vanished as the door thudded shut.

The moment the light disappeared he worked swiftly. His arm moved under the loosened ropes. His hand groped for the pocket, his fingers closed about the knife. He drew it out. There was enough leeway that he was able to turn his wrist and get the sharp blade against one of the strands of rope.

"One bullet won't do it!" growled Sailor Skene. "Two bullets won't do it, either. I'm going to use them all, mister, and you'll still be living when I'm ready to use the last one."

He pushed Delaney roughly ahead of him. "Feel your way down that path!" he ordered.

Delaney hacked and slashed feverishly at the rope. The knife, fortunately, had a blade like a razor. He felt the strands give. The ropes fell free. But Skene's gun was still at his back, and he knew that Skene's finger was on the trigger.

He pretended to stumble. With his arms still close at his sides, Delaney reeled and went to his knees in the snow.

Skene kicked him. "Come on. Get up!"

Delaney managed to turn as he struggled to his feet. Crouching, he could see the Sailor's burly figure in the gloom, dark against the snow.

Then he sprang.

Delaney's arm flashed out as he came up. Sailor Skene, confident in the belief that his victim was tightly bound, was totally unprepared for the swinging thrust, for the hand that closed on the barrel of the gun and wrenched it halfway out of his grip.

Skene uttered a startled yell, and in the next moment Delaney had closed with him. But Skene's wild, instinctive lunge had knocked the knife from Delaney's grasp. It fell into the snow. They fought for the gun.

Delaney's right came up with jolting force as he drove Skene a terrific blow against the jaw. Skene's head went back, but he clung doggedly to the butt of the revolver, tried desperately to work his finger beneath the trigger guard again. Delaney twisted viciously at the gun. Skene, fighting back, smashed him between the eyes.

Delaney rushed his opponent, driving him back into the deep snow beside the path. Skene floundered, his arm high and rigid as he tried to break Delaney's grip on the weapon. Delaney wrenched suddenly and tore the gun from Skene's grasp.

He could have fired and finished Sailor Skene then and there, but he wanted no shots to disturb the camp. If there was to be any hope of escape, it must lie in the speed and silence of the get-away. He dodged two frantic blows as Skene swung at him desperately, and then he smashed the barrel of the gun squarely against the Sailor's temple.

Skene gasped and reeled, but he wasn't out yet. Delaney staggered him with a right-hand jolt to the face and brought the gun down again. It thudded dully against the big man's skull. Skene collapsed like an empty sack. He went down without a groan, knocked senseless.

Delaney didn't know whether Skene was dead or

alive. It was enough for him that he was free, that he had a loaded gun in his hand, and that the man lay motionless in the snow at his feet.

Now things were different!

He raced silently up the path, back toward the cabin. The camp was silent. Lights gleamed in the windows of some of the cabins. But his battle with Sailor Skene had been so brief and so quiet that no one had been aroused.

As he approached Blackjack Adler's door he heard sobs, a muffled scream, sounds of a struggle, and the old pirate's laughter.

Dan Delaney crashed against the door. It swung swiftly open before him, and he stood there on the threshold, crouching, gun in hand.

Blackjack Adler, struggling with Jean in his arms, swung around, his face contorted with surprise.

"Up, Adler!" jerked Delaney. "Up with them or I'll put a bullet through you!"

Jean tore herself from Adler's grasp with a frantic sob of relief. As for the old outlaw, he stared at Delaney with an expression of wild incredulity. Then he stumbled back, his arms rising slowly.

Delaney strode into the cabin as Jean flung herself into his arms. Over her shoulder he watched Adler. His finger trembled on the trigger. There was death in his eyes, and Adler knew it. But Delaney knew that a shot now would bring the whole camp down about his ears.

"Come on, Adler!" he snapped. "We're going now. One yell for help, and I'll fill you full of lead."

Blackjack Adler had held too many men helpless at the point of a gun not to know desperation when he saw it. He knew that a false move meant his death.

"You're going to set the others free, Adler! And you're going to do it quietly. If any of your men try to block this get-away, you'll get the first bullet. Understand that?"

Adler frowned. "And what then?" he demanded. "You can't get out of the valley."

"You'll see. We're taking your plane, Adler!"

The outlaw was staggered. An expression of dismay flashed into his eyes. Delaney gave him no time to recover.

"That was your ace in the hole, Adler! But we're taking it, and I'll be at the controls. You and your gang are marooned here until the Mounties come for you. Quick! Get moving!"

He drove the outlaw before him at the point of the gun, and, with arms still raised, Blackjack Adler stumbled across the threshold out into the night. The outlaw was silent, but Delaney knew that the cunning old brain was working swiftly.

Adler, he knew, would be dangerous to the last. Delaney took no chances with the man. He bade Jean get her parka from the cabin and follow quickly. Then he stayed close at Adler's heels as the outlaw lurched down the trail.

They passed the prostrate body of Sailor Skene, black against the snow. They halted before one of the tiny cabins.

"The keys," snapped the Snow Hawk.

Adler hesitated.

"The keys are in my pocket," he muttered.

Delaney thrust the gun hard against the outlaw's body and searched him. He found the keys, swiftly picked out one that fitted the padlock on the door. Then his heart jumped.

A bright rectangle of light fell suddenly across the snow. The door of one of the other cabins opened. A man stood there, silhouetted against the light, peering out into the darkness.

"Who's there?" he called. It was the voice of Krug.

Delaney jammed the gun barrel savagely into Adler's ribs. The outlaw growled: "It's only me, Krug. It's all right."

"Okay, chief!" Krug went back in and closed the door.

Delaney breathed easier. He unsnapped the padlock and kicked open the door. He heard his father's voice, startled, call out from the darkness within: "What's that? Is someone—"

"Get Doug!" he said sharply. "Hurry! It's the get-away!"

He could see Jean hurrying down the path. In less than three minutes his father and young MacLean were stumbling out of the cabin, ready for flight. They asked no questions. It was enough for them that the apparently impossible had happened and that the way was paved for their escape from this valley of dread.

Away down on the valley floor, a dark blot against the snow, they could see the gloomy shape of the great plane. With Blackjack Adler sullenly trudging ahead, the revolver thrust into the small of his back, the fugitives hastened down the slope.

Delaney knew that the most ticklish part of the business was yet to come. The engine would be cold. It might be difficult to start. And every passing minute increased the possibility of discovery.

Down in the shadow of the great wings he saw that the cowling of the machine was covered with tarpaulin. He turned to his father, thrust the gun into his hands.

"Cover him!" he ordered. Then to Jean: "Climb into the cabin. You'll be safer there if trouble starts." To Doug MacLean: "Give me a hand."

MacLean tore the tarpaulin away and Delaney scrambled into the pilot's seat. On his flight with Koleff and Gilstrom he had seen that the plant was equipped with a self-starter, but he knew that time would be needed to warm up the engine. He switched on the ignition.

From the hillside came a shout. Lights were flashing. Their escape had been noticed. Through the night Delaney heard the bull-like roar of Sailor Skene:

"Get the guns! They're down at the plane now!"

He worked desperately at the mechanism, but at first there was no response. The uproar on the hillside grew louder. Suddenly the engine caught, spluttered, broke into a roar. Every second was precious now. He could see dark shadows against the snow, men running down the slope.

Matt Delaney yelled in Adler's ear: "If one of them comes down here shooting, I'll drop you!" But only Adler heard him, for the roar of the motor drowned his words. Adler began shouting at the approaching men, ordering them to stay back, but they could not hear him and came plunging on.

Up on the slope a rifle blazed. The motor was thundering now. A bullet went whining past one of the wings. Delaney yelled at his father and young MacLean. They scrambled up onto the wing and into the cabin.

Blackjack Adler broke into a run, waving his arms and shouting at his men. Delaney drew back the throttle slowly. The plane lurched, the skis grated on the frozen snow, and then the great machine moved.

Chapter 16:

Night Flight

The outlaws, however, were only a few yards away now. A gun blazed and a bullet smacked through the cabin window. Matt Delaney answered the fire, and one of the dark figures went plunging into the snow. The plane slid away with maddening slowness.

A great burly figure came plunging from the clump of men, sprang, and scratched the wing. Skene was crawling up onto the wing as the machine picked up speed and went sliding out across the white floor.

Skene crouched on the wing, and his arm went up. A revolver blazed. The plane was gathering speed now, lurching as it thundered off across the frozen surface. Matt Delaney fired twice through the cabin window, but Skene was an unsteady target as he came crawling along the wing. The other outlaws were far behind now, and the plane was roaring across the flat.

Out of the corner of his eye Delaney could see Skene clinging to one of the struts, trying to steady himself for a shot. He took a chance on his air speed. The plane seemed to falter—and then took off. The skis rose from the snow. The roar of Skene's gun was almost drowned, but Delaney saw the flash. The lurch had thrown Skene off-balance. The bullet went wide.

The machine was rising now. Delaney could see the great, grim barrier of mountain ahead. He had to get altitude. He brought the nose of the plane up steadily. Skene was out of sight now, down on the wing. Delaney banked. The white floor of snow was receding.

A head rose slowly above the level of the shattered window. He had a glimpse of Skene's evil face, of a leveled gun. Delaney sent the plane into a dive, then brought the nose up sharply and climbed.

The head vanished. Even above the roar of the motor Delaney heard the last wild cry of terror as Skene was flung clear of the wing and sent hurtling to his death, a spinning figure in the night, plunging to the snowy floor of Killer's Valley.

And so, in a gradually widening spiral, the big plane rose higher and higher, climbing toward the icy stars until at last Delaney straightened it out and the machine shot roaring over the mountains.

There was a full moon in the sky, flooding the ice-locked land with light. Off in the distance to the west he could see the winding ribbon of the Bitter River, as the plane went throbbing high above the ice-locked wilderness toward the south.

Suddenly the steady roar of the engine was broken. It missed, barked, broke forth anew, flames spurting.

Engine trouble! Delaney's heart jumped. His hand gripped the stick convulsively. Engine trouble meant but one thing—a forced landing. Delaney grinned and made an encouraging gesture. He knew they were not fooled. They realized the danger as well as he did. The Snow Hawk was not a first-class pilot. He was a good amateur, but no more than that.

The steady beat of the motor faltered once more. The plane lurched, began to stall. Delaney shoved the nose over and flung the ship into a dive. It went howling toward the ground. At last the engine picked up again, crashed out anew.

Gradually Delaney pulled back on the stick, brought the plane out of that vicious dive. The machine quaked and quivered under the terrific strain. The engine faltered, stuttered sluggishly and died.

Delaney's mouth was set in a tight line. He sat back

and gestured resignedly. "We're going to land," he said. "Hold on, everyone." The words were scarcely out of his mouth before there was a brief, momentary shock. A violent shudder ran through the plane.

Delaney brought the nose of the ship up quickly. Treetops! The plane was skimming over bush country.

Another rending crash. Something grabbed one of the wings and yanked the plane sideways.

Delaney yelled at Jean and with one swift motion thrust her down below the window level. There was a terrific crashing, jolting, and bumping. Glass was breaking all around him. He was flung violently to one side as the ship keeled over. There was one final jarring shock—and then silence.

Dan Delaney, numb, bruised, and shaken, conscious that blood was streaming from a cut in his forehead, groped for Jean.

"Everybody okay?" he asked, trying to keep his voice steady. His heart was chilled with fear lest there should be no response.

"I'm all right, son," came his father's voice, weak and strained. "Shook up a bit, but I'm all right."

"Boy!" exclaimed Doug MacLean fervently. "Were the angels watching me? Not a scratch!"

But Jean did not speak. He found her, motionless and silent, huddled against the side of the cabin. The machine was canted at a sharp angle. "Jean!"

Still that dreadful silence. Delaney picked her up in his arms. She was breathing. Doug was wrenching and hammering at the cabin door, jammed by the crash. He broke it open at last. They struggled out into the snow, down over the slanting side of the plane, Delaney carrying her in his arms.

Old Matt Delaney, after several futile efforts, groaned and remained where he was.

"Don't worry about me," he muttered. "I just can't seem to move one of my legs. Feels broken."

Delaney and young MacLean were waist-deep in snow under the broken trees. Matt flung a fur robe out of the plane and they laid the girl upon it, clearing away some of the snow. In the flickering light of a match Delaney saw that she had a dark bruise on her forehead, where she had evidently hit the instrument panel.

Their fears that she might have suffered a fractured skull were set at rest in a few minutes, however, when Jean's eyelids flickered, and she looked up at them.

"You're not hurt!" exclaimed Delaney.

Jean tried to smile. "My head . . . "

The match in Delaney's hand flickered and went out. The wind howled through the trees. Snow was falling on the wreckage of the plane. Their lives had been spared—but for how long? Marooned in the Northern wilderness, without dogs, the plane a crumpled heap of débris, lost and without food, the future was black.

Morning broke with bleak skies and biting cold that seemed to strike to the bone.

In the gray gloom of daybreak the refugees huddled beside a roaring fire under the trees. The flames leaped toward the snow-laden branches of the spruce. The black tree trunks and the dark-green branches of the forest stood out clearly against the white background.

The one grotesque note was the wreck of the plane. It lay on its side, one wing crumpled to matchwood beneath it, the other wing projecting high in the air with the torn fabric hanging in strips from the framework. The nose of the ship was buried deep in the snow.

There, in the shadow of the wrecked plane, they took stock of the situation. Matt Delaney, wrapped in blankets found in the plane, lay with his broken leg bound in improvised splints.

"A clean break," his son had said, tending to the fractured limb. "It will take a while to mend, but you'll walk again. You're lucky, dad!"

"Can't see anything lucky about it," grumbled the

old man, "unless you mean I'm lucky it wasn't my neck I broke instead of my leg. I'm going to be a burden to everybody, instead of being able to help." He gnawed at his white mustache in exasperation and his blue eyes were anxious. "How are you going to get out of this mess—with a cripple on your hands?"

Matt Delaney, in spite of the fact that he was an old man, chafed at the injury. He was a veteran of the gold trails, a man to whom the wilderness was an open book. That he, of the four, should be the only one helpless to fight against the trap into which they had fallen made him furious with resentment.

"What can we do, Dan?" asked Jean. "Have you any idea where we are?"

"Not the slightest," he told her. "We are somewhere between the northern boundary of Alberta and the Thunder Mountain Range, somewhere between the Mackenzie River and the Hudson Bay country."

"That's a lot of territory," commented Doug Mac-Lean. "Do you think we can get out?"

Delaney shrugged. "With luck, we'll make it. And I feel lucky." He patted the soft fur of the white parka he was wearing. "I found this in the plane."

Delaney's pleasure at finding the white parka in the cabin was natural. With it he was again the Snow Hawk.

"Let's check our assets," he said.

"We are alive," said Jean.

"And we have a revolver, a rifle, an ax, a pair of snowshoes, matches, and a compass," remarked Doug. The snowshoes, ax, and rifle had been found in the cabin of the plane, evidently kept there by Adler's pilot in case of emergency.

"We also know that Blackjack Adler and his crew are marooned back in the valley," Delaney said.

"Don't be too sure of that," growled Matt.

"But we took their plane."

"We took one plane. They have another."

Delaney frowned. This was news to him. He had seen but the one ship during his stay in Killer's Valley, and he had taken it for granted that the outlaws had been left without means of escape from their mountain prison.

"That's right," said Doug gloomily. "They have another machine. It wasn't used much. Adler wouldn't be fool enough to risk everything with one machine. If Koleff, the pilot, had ever been forced down outside the valley, Adler would have been in a fine jam."

Delaney bit his lip. "That's a liability, then. You can depend on it, Adler will be looking for us. He has the map of the gold find, but it's of no use to him as long as we're alive. So he'll come."

"He will start out in the plane," said Matt slowly, "and if he chances to come this way, if he sees us here —we've had it."

"If we only had dogs and a sled!" Doug exclaimed.

"We'll get them," Delaney said.

He knew that any flight to civilization was impossible without dogs. His father was unable to walk, even if they were willing to undertake the terrible hardship of a journey on foot through the trackless snows.

"There is only one way out," he added. "Someone will have to go for help."

There was a dead silence. They all knew the tremendous obstacles and deadly risks confronting any one who ventured alone and on foot into the wilderness.

After a while Delaney said quietly: "I'll go." He knew that he might never live to return. And if he died, his companions were doomed. The responsibility rested on his shoulders.

Chapter 17:
Journey into the Wilderness

His head bowed to the biting wind, his snowshoes kicking up little flurries of snow at every step, Delaney trudged down the white path of a frozen creek. He had been going for hours, which seemed like days. The surface of the creek afforded an open trail. It would, he knew, eventually bring him to a lake or river. By staying to the watercourses he would have a better chance of coming upon a cabin or encampment.

Swinging down the creek he thought of the three people he had left in the makeshift camp in the bush. His jaw set grimly. They must be saved. After all the risks he had taken it was inconceivable that a mere accident should toss victory to Blackjack Adler.

There was a faint rustle in the bush behind him. Delaney looked back. He heard a slight crackling noise. Then a ghostly shadow flitted among the tree trunks on the bank of the creek.

The shadow vanished.

Delaney felt the hair bristling at his temples and on the back of his neck. The bush was silent, apparently deserted. Was there something in the woods, or was his imagination playing tricks on him?

He went on a few more paces. He heard a soft shuffle of snow dislodged from the lower branches of a balsam. His ears were attuned to the faintest sound.

Swiftly, he wheeled and looked back again.

Delaney saw nothing out of the way. But now he was sure. Now he knew that something was watching him from the shelter of the trees.

Delaney turned and went on again. There was a bend in the winding waterway ahead. When he went around the bend he stopped and waited, watching the back trail.

A gaunt, gray shape flitted swiftly into view.

The animal saw Delaney standing there. It wheeled and vanished like a flash, but not before two others came loping silently in its wake. They were gone in an instant.

Delaney's mouth twisted in a wry grin. "Wolves!" he muttered.

The brutes were hungry. They had picked up his trail. They would follow him now, silently and relentlessly. Delaney examined his revolver, broke it, saw that the chambers were loaded, thrust it back into his pocket.

"About as much use as a popgun against that pack!" he said.

He turned, lowered his head, and went on.

In spite of himself his skin prickled with the knowledge of those spectral shadows on his trail. The gaunt brutes were shy now, but they would become bolder. He knew that it had been fool-hardy to set out on this trail without the rifle—but what else could be done? The others would starve without the weapon.

Delaney did not look back again. He knew that the wolves were still trailing him. The creek widened out, and he found himself approaching the white, unbroken surface of a small lake.

At the southern end of the lake he saw an opening—the frozen roadway of a river. Delaney struck out for it. When he was far out on the ice he looked back again.

Five black shapes came skulking in his tracks. They were about half a mile behind. They stopped, sat on their haunches. One of them raised its nose to the sky.

Out across the lake rang a dreary, blood-curdling howl. It echoed mournfully in the immense silence that overhung the wilderness.

Then, from far beyond the ridge of hills, Delaney heard an answering cry. It was immediately followed by a chorus of long-drawn howls, the terrifying chorus of a second wolf pack on the trail.

The surface of the ridge was bare and rocky. He could see it clearly in the distance. A moment later, on the sloping hillside, he saw a moving black speck against the white background. It was followed by another and another, and all the time the fiendish chorus grew louder. The pack swept down the slope. Fleet as the wind, they were racing toward the lake.

Delaney swung into his tireless pace across the ice again. He was heading for the river. That weird chorus behind him had power to shake the strongest nerves. It was fearful and unforgettable. He fought down a rising panic—the dreaded wolf panic that gnaws insidiously at a man's courage until he loses his nerve and flees, blindly, exhausting his strength.

By the time he reached the river the two wolf packs had joined. Now a dozen of them were silently following the long line of tracks across the ice.

He left the lake behind and went trudging down the river. When he glanced back again he saw that the wolves had become bolder. They were slowly closing the gap. The leader, a huge black wolf, trotted well in advance of the pack.

Delaney quickened his speed, although he knew he could not hope to outrace them. The giant king of the pack was eating up the distance.

He threaded his way among the hummocks, knowing that only a thin sheet of ice lay between himself and swiftly rushing water. A dark patch showed about an air hole. He skirted it carefully.

Crack!

The ice heaved. The noise was followed by a succession of splintering crashes. Delaney felt one snowshoe sink. Brittle ice broke beneath his weight. He leaped and fell. He lay flat for one agonizing moment, but the ice held. Slowly he crawled forward.

A howl had gone up from the king wolf. Then the whole pack joined in. They were in full cry. Delaney looked back to see them racing down the river. Their caution was gone. The quarry was down, and the wolves were rushing in for the kill.

Delaney scrambled to his feet. The wolves spread out. Some of the more timid slowed up. But the king wolf raced on. Delaney whipped out his revolver and fired.

The king wolf swerved and leaped to one side. A gaunt brute only a few feet behind uttered a fiendish yelp, sprang into the air, and came down writhing. With a savage chorus of yelps the pack sprang upon him. The air was hideous with the sounds of the feast.

Delaney struggled on, his revolver still gripped in his hand. He stumbled over a boulder rising above the ice and fell again. He crawled painfully to his feet and saw that half a dozen of the wolves were racing toward him. He fired twice. The wolves scattered. His shot had not taken effect, but the gunfire checked their headlong rush. They skulked back, eying him. He sighted at the king wolf, who was circling in the snow, snarling, and pulled the trigger.

The gun jammed!

Clogged with snow when he had fallen, now it failed him when he needed it most. Desperately, he worked at the mechanism, pried at the frozen snow about the hammer. The king wolf was sidling in, its ears flat, its red-rimmed eyes ferocious. It slithered toward him through the snow, advancing for the spring.

Delaney got to his feet. The wolves were in a huge semicircle before him, but some were skulking around, trying to get behind him. He backed away, struggling with the gun.

They seemed to sense that he was unarmed now. The king wolf came in with a rush, slashing viciously with a sidewise chop of bared fangs as it went by. Delaney swung and struck it across the head with the gun barrel. He saw one of the other brutes race around behind him.

He retreated toward the river bank, trying to get the sheer rock wall at his back. But the king wolf was swinging around, sidling in again. It raced at him. Delaney lunged back. His snowshoes became entangled; he staggered and then fell.

As he sank into the snow he could see the swiftly moving shapes as the wolf pack swept in upon their prey.

Chapter 18:
Retreat into Danger

There was a sharp, ringing sound like a hammer striking an anvil. It echoed suddenly in the frosty air.

The Snow Hawk, floundering in the snow, his heart gripped with despair as he faced the ravenous pack surging down on him, heard that sound. In the same instant he saw the king wolf tumble in a heap.

The rest of the pack scattered in wild alarm and confusion. They bolted in all directions, yelping with terror. Another distant rifle shot sounded above the clamor.

The pack was flung into instant panic. The rifle spoke again and again. But by this time the wolves were in full flight. They scuttled through the snow, racing to escape the fate that had struck at their comrades from a clear sky.

Delaney rose to his feet. He was stunned by this swift and unexpected deliverance from what had seemed certain death.

Two hundred yards away, on a high rock overlooking the bend in the river, a dark figure moved. It was a man. Rifle in hand, he scrambled down from the rock to the ice and then trudged toward Delaney.

As they approached each other the Snow Hawk saw that he was a tall, thin fellow with melancholy eyes and a scraggly black beard—a middle-aged man in a patched and moth-eaten parka.

"Looks as if I just happened along in time," drawled the stranger, shifting the rifle in the crook of his arm. His eyes were fixed on the Snow Hawk with a curiously intense stare.

"I would have been done for," said Delaney simply.

He extended his hand.

The other man shrugged. "Wolves!" he muttered. "Don't often hear of them going after a man. Of course, that pack was hungry—and you're traveling alone." There was a questioning note in his voice. Then he said: "How come you're on the trail without a rifle?"

"It's a long story," said Delaney. "I came out to get help—some friends of mine camped back in the bush—plane crash. Is your cabin near here? If I can get shelter and food I'll tell you how it happened."

The stranger's eyes traveled slowly over Delaney's white parka. "There's a camp just around the bend," he said. "My name's Ned Price."

Delaney nodded. The name of Ned Price was familiar to him. Hunter, trapper, trader, this lanky man had lived in the wilderness all his life. Then, seeing that Ned Price was glancing at him expectantly, he said:

"My name is Delaney."

"Yeah?" said Price. There was something vaguely disturbing in his tone.

About half a mile beyond the bend in the river lay a small group of huts and cabins. It was a shabby little encampment. Ragged youngsters were playing in the snow. A dozen mongrel dogs rushed out yelping.

Delaney received a distinct and unpleasant shock when two men emerged from one of the cabins and advanced to meet them. One of the men, a truculent-looking fellow with fierce eyes, stared at him in obvious hostility. He lunged forward, his eyes glaring hatred. His hand flew to the knife in his belt.

"None of that!" growled Ned Price, stepping in front of Delaney, letting loose an explosive flow of curses. The man shrugged and stood submissively in the snow.

"What's the trouble?" asked Delaney.

Ned Price did not answer. "Come into my shack,"

he said, "and get yourself dried out."

Delaney was bewildered by the attitude of the strange man. Later, as he sat by Price's fire, he came back to the subject again.

"What was the matter with that fellow?" he demanded. "He looked as if he was going to draw a knife on me."

Ned Price puffed calmly at his pipe. "He was."

"He was?" cried Delaney, astonished. "But why?"

Ned Price pointed with his pipe at Delaney's white parka, hanging on the wall.

"That!" he said.

Then Delaney knew. He had been recognized as the Snow Hawk. But even then he could not understand the reason for the man's hostile attitude. There had been murder in the fellow's eyes.

"So!" he replied calmly. "But why the knife? I have never harmed him."

"You killed his son," answered Ned Price gravely.

Delaney was momentarily dumbfounded. He stared at Price in utter consternation.

"It's lucky I was here," said the trapper. "If you had walked into this camp alone, Tom Brooks would have cut your throat the minute he clapped eyes on that white parka of yours."

"But I didn't kill his son!" snapped Delaney. "This is the first time I've ever been in this part of the country."

"You were seen." Price shook his head. "I'll go as far as to keep Tom Brooks from taking revenge on you, but I won't go any farther. You're wanted by the Mounties, from what we've heard. We're going to bring you south and turn you over to them."

"But look here!" cried Delaney desperately. "I haven't told you my story yet. I came out to get help for three people who are marooned north of here in the bush. One of them is my father, and he has a broken leg. I've got to get a dog team to bring him out. The others are MacLean's son and daughter from Lonely Lake."

Swiftly, tensely, he told Ned Price of the affair at Killer's Valley, of their escape the previous night, the crash, and his decision to set out in search of help.

Price listened skeptically. "It's too thin," he grunted at last. "You want a dog team, eh? You want us to fit you out with a sled and dogs and off you go." He laughed scornfully. "Nothing doing. And as for that— story about the outlaws and your airplane and all the rest of it—I don't believe a word of it."

"Come with me, then!" argued Delaney. "Come with me. We can make it in a few hours. You'll find I'm telling the truth."

Ned Price considered this reflectively. But before he could reply, the door was thrust open.

Tom Brooks stood on the threshold. Behind him crowded half a dozen men, their faces stern. Brooks stepped into the cabin, his arms folded. Ned Price repeated Delaney's story to the group, but it was clear that they didn't believe a word of it.

"It's all right with me if you're taken south right away to be hanged for killing my son," growled Tom Brooks, "but I won't go further than that."

"These outlaws have committed many crimes that have been blamed on me. One of these men killed your son. And I will see that the man is turned over to the police. My friends will starve to death unless help comes to them at once."

The men were scornful. The Snow Hawk, to them, was an outlaw, a killer, a man who was not to be trusted for a moment. Tom Brooks disposed of the argument with a few curt words and then folded his arms again, ominously determined.

"It won't work," said Ned Price to Delaney.

Far off in the distance, Delaney heard a sound like the humming of a bee. It became steadily louder. The men exchanged questioning glances. One of them turned and went outside, looking up toward the sky.

Delaney's face went white. Adler's plane!

Delaney swung around to face Ned Price. "There's the proof!" he shouted. "That's Adler's plane. And if he spots that wrecked plane my friends are done for."

Tom Brooks growled something to Ned Price. The trapper said: "Even if it is true, they don't want to get mixed up in any gun fight with outlaws. You're going south, mister."

Delaney was furious. It was maddening to think that he was helpless. There was a strange irony of fate in the whole situation. The evil reputation that the Snow Hawk had built up for himself as a disguise had become a trap that gripped him at the very time he needed aid.

He argued, pleaded, stormed. Ned Price was unmoved. The trapper had lived with these men for years, and he knew that in this case it was not wise to interfere. Tom Brook's son had been killed, and the Snow Hawk was suspected as the murderer.

"You're lucky to be going south, at that," growled Price. "If it wasn't for me, Tom Brooks would appoint himself judge, jury, and executioner right now."

"Well, then, send some of the men over my back trail for my friends!" exclaimed Delaney desperately. "Every one of them may be shot down in cold blood if they don't get help."

Ned Price scratched his ear reflectively and spat into the snow. "I'll send one of the boys up tomorrow."

"Tomorrow! But that may be too late. *One* man! Send them all."

"And have them all wiped out by a gang of murderers?" He had not been greatly impressed by Delaney's story. The Snow Hawk, he believed, was unscrupulous, a man to be watched, not to be trusted on any account.

Delaney saw that argument was useless. He would have to get out of this jam by using his wits—force, if necessary.

"All right," he said, apparently submissive. "I'm licked. But you'll learn, Price, that I haven't been lying. I didn't kill the boy. The Mounties don't want me."

He turned as if about to go back into the cabin. One of the men was standing near the doorway, a rifle in the crook of his arm. Several of the men were carrying guns, and Delaney knew that any bid for escape meant risking swift and sudden death from a bullet.

When he was a few feet away from Brooks he turned and again spoke to Price:

"If those people back there are killed, *you'll* have to do some explaining to the Mounties. Don't say I didn't warn you of—"

And then, like a striking rattler, his arm shot out, and he lunged sideways. He had wrenched the rifle out of the man's grasp before the fellow's slow wits realized his intention. One swift, sudden motion and Delaney had them covered. They were stunned, taken completely off guard.

"Now!" shouted Delaney. "Hitch up those dogs!"

Chapter 19:

Escape

The Snow Hawk held the whip hand. The rifle covered every man in the group. No one moved.

"Put down that gun," warned Ned Price in a low voice. "You'll never get away with it."

"Hitch up a team and be quick about it."

Delaney's voice was harsh and imperative. His eyes were like ice. The trapper hesitated a moment and then gave in.

Tom Brook's face was livid with hatred. His hand had closed on the knife in his belt, but he dared not draw the blade.

"You've settled your beef now, mister," said Price. "Steal those dogs and the Mounties will be holding an inquest instead of a trial."

"I'll take my chances," snapped Delaney. "I've told you my story, and it's true. If anything happens to me, you'll have to answer for it."

One of the men was hitching up the dogs "Price!" Delaney said. "I want some grub. And I want ammunition for this gun—"

Whi-o-ing!

A bullet skimmed within inches of Delaney's head. He caught sight of a movement at the back of one of the cabins, saw a rifle barrel projecting around the end logs of the building. The dogs, frightened, plunged wildly. Delaney flung himself on the sled just as the animals bolted down the trail toward the river.

Ned Price and the others were dodging across the open space in front of the shacks, heading for their weapons. Doors slammed. Delaney flung himself around on the sled; the dogs were racing down the back trail across the ice.

Delaney briefly saw Ned Price and Tom Brooks run to hitch up another team. Brooks, intent upon revenge, was not letting the Snow Hawk escape so easily. By the time his own dogs went swinging around the bend, the second team was hitting the trail.

At the back of Delaney's mind hammered the knowledge that Adler's plane had passed almost directly over the bush where his companions were waiting. Only a miracle could have saved them from observation. He might be too late.

While the Snow Hawk was racing northward in the fading light, Jean MacLean and Matt Delaney were enduring tortures of uncertainty beside the fire in the heart of the bush. The flames leaped and flickered in the great shadow of the wrecked plane. Matt, lying helpless on a pallet of pine boughs, clenched his fists in exasperation.

"If I could only do something!" he groaned. "We shouldn't have let Dan go. Might have known those fellows would find us."

For they had been found.

Blackjack Adler's plane had passed high over the bush, half an hour before. It had droned on and passed out of sight. For a while it had seemed that they were safe. But the plane had returned, this time flying low, skimming over the treetops. And then it had circled around to come to a landing on the surface of a lake on the edge of the forest.

MacLean, taking the rifle that was their only weapon, had set out toward the lake. He knew that they would die.

When he judged that he was about halfway to the lake he slackened his pace and became more cautious. The Snow Hawk, on his way out that morning, had left a clear trail in the snow. It would not take long for Adler and his men to pick up that track. They would know that it would lead them directly to the camp in the bush.

MacLean proceeded carefully, picking his way from tree to tree, his eyes fixed on that straggling line of snowshoe tracks ahead. But at last, when he came within sight of the lake and caught a glimpse of the black hulk of Adler's plane beyond the trees, he knew that the outlaws had outwitted him. They had expected an ambush on that tempting trail.

Suddenly, over to the left, he heard a snapping of twigs, a crackling in the bushes. Then he heard voices.

MacLean could see no one, but he wheeled about and went back on the trail. The men had been abreast of him, about a hundred yards away. He loped silently beneath the snow-laden branches. He had to keep between the enemy and the camp.

It was a forlorn hope, and he knew it. He might be lucky enough to account for one of the outlaws, but his first shot would draw the fire of the others upon him. These men had come out upon a mission of murder, well armed and fully equipped. He had but one rifle and six shells.

In the deep bush he knew that the outlaws would make slower progress than he could make on the broken trail. They were probably equipped with snowshoes, but there would be fallen trees and heavy undergrowth to bar their way. When he judged that he was well ahead of them, MacLean struck out into the deep snow off the trail and made his way to a dense covert of balsam. He crouched among the trees and waited, peering into the silent and sinister forest.

After a while he heard the sharp snap of a broken branch. The sound electrified him. His nerves were tense as he raised the rifle and gazed at the bush in the direction of the noise. Here was danger!

"Keep well apart!" called a gruff voice. "Spread out and stay away from that trail. We've got to go slow and easy now. No more noise."

"Okay, chief!" returned another voice, from some distance over to the right.

MacLean could not see either of the speakers as yet for the bush was very thick. Then, from around a clump of evergreen, emerged a dark-clad figure.

It was Blackjack Adler.

MacLean squinted down the rifle barrel and drew a bead on the outlaw.

Neither he nor his companions could expect mercy from Adler. The man could expect no mercy from him.

But the evil good luck that had followed Blackjack Adler through all his years of crime had not deserted him. Just as MacLean's finger pressed the trigger—a fraction of a second before the shot rang out—Adler lurched suddenly, plunged off-balance, and fell sprawling over a dead tree that lay in his path.

The crash of MacLean's rifle echoed through the woods. Swiftly he sighted down on the plunging figure in the snow. But he was shaken by his failure. Perhaps, too, some instinct against shooting a man who was not on his feet made MacLean's trigger finger tremble. Whatever the reason, when he fired again he missed, and by that time Blackjack Adler had twisted around. Lying in the snow, the outlaw wriggled back to cover behind the dead tree, and in the next instant his rifle was spitting flame and lead.

Only the fact that MacLean was well hidden by the evergreen thicket saved his life. He crouched, breathless, under a veritable hurricane of bullets. But Adler was shooting high. MacLean flattened out and crawled beneath the lowest branches, got out of the line of fire. Then, when the attack ended, he scrambled up, sought the shelter of another tree, got back into the deep bush and darted in behind a great fallen pine where the heavy branches provided a thick screen.

Dead silence hung over the bush now.

"They'll know it isn't going to be a pushover, anyway," muttered MacLean grimly.

But he had lost the first round. The outlaws knew of his presence. He had lost the advantage of the first shot and had gained nothing. Even yet he did not know how many men were in the party.

Some secret warning of danger bade him look around. He caught a glimpse of a dark figure standing erect behind the cover of a tree trunk. A rifle was leveled. The man was coolly taking aim.

MacLean jerked back frantically just as the rifle spoke. The bullet knocked splinters from the dead bough that had been beyond his head a moment before. He dropped down behind the screen of branches and dived beneath the heavy trunk.

There he found an opening, saw the man peering out from behind the tree. The enemy was sure he had scored a hit. MacLean heard him shout: "Got him!" It was Koleff's voice.

There was an answering shout from among the trees over on the other side.

MacLean poked the nose of his gun clear of the branches under the tree trunk and fired.

He saw Koleff lurch suddenly behind the tree. The man's rifle dropped into the snow. MacLean saw an arm swing around and encircle the tree for support as Koleff clung there.

He did not know if he had wounded the pilot fatally or not. A moment later there was another burst of gunfire to his right, and bullets began thudding into the trunk of the dead pine.

MacLean knew that the thick screen of branches sheltered him from view on that side, but one of those random shots might easily find him. He crawled back, retreated slowly from the big tree, taking advantage of every bit of cover, and got back into the deeper bush.

It was quite dark in among the trees. Twilight was beginning to close in on the forest, and in a little while he knew he would be unable to see his enemies. But that would give them the advantage. He knew that there were at least three of them and perhaps more. If one of those men came upon Jean and old Matt they would be utterly without protection.

MacLean knew he had to find his way back to the camp. If he got too far away from the trail he would be lost. It would be easy enough to save his own life—but only at the expense of the others.

He waited for some movement, some noise that would indicate the location of Adler and his men. But there was not a sound. The forest was wrapped in a cold, stern silence.

The outlaws were going to wait him out.

They could afford to wait. They had the numbers, the arms, and the ammunition. Coolly, they were waiting for darkness. Then they would close in for the kill.

MacLean backed away through the bush, making no sound in the deep snow. He struck out toward the trail again. After ten minutes, with twilight steadily growing deeper, he was still in the heavy timber; he had not found the trail.

Half an hour later, blundering through the darkness, crashing into trees, stumbling over logs, he sank down exhausted in the snow. He was lost. And in his half-frozen hands was clutched the rifle—the only weapon that could save the lives of Jean MacLean and the Snow Hawk's father.

Chapter 20:
The Final Showdown

The dogs were weary. The Snow Hawk had driven them hard, sparing neither the animals nor himself on that wild dash from the camp.

The welcoming shadows of the forest drew nearer and nearer. Two rifles blazed from the sled behind as Tom Brooks and Price realized that the fugitive would have the advantage once the bush swallowed him up. The bullets whistled dangerously near. And then, with a last despairing effort, Delaney stumbled up the rocky shore and staggered into the darkness of the bush.

He turned, panting. He could scarcely raise the rifle as he leaned against a tree and aimed above the oncoming dogs. He fired—once.

The dogs veered. There was a wild scramble as the two men leaped from the sled, one to each side, and took shelter behind it.

"You'll think twice before you come ahead now," Delaney muttered. Then he struck out down the trail.

He ejected the empty shell from his gun. But no shell snapped into the breech to replace it.

The rifle was empty. And in the forest ahead were enemies far more ruthless than the ones he had left behind.

Blackjack Adler and his men did not know that the marksman who had given them such an unpleasant ten minutes on the trail was now wandering lost in the darkness of the bush. His spirited stand had made them hesitate. The very fact that his gun had not been heard again made them cautious. They had held a council of war.

Koleff, his left shoulder bound up with cloth torn hastily from his shirt to stanch the flow of blood from a bullet wound, was in favor of making camp until daylight. Brown and Peterson were in favor of going on while there was still light enough to follow the trail.

"Get it over with!" snapped Peterson. "We can go in there and wipe 'em out in five minutes."

Blackjack Adler was not afraid of risks, but he believed in minimizing them.

"If we camp," he growled, "we must have a fire. That's no good. We'd be shot down. When it's dark we can follow that trail in. I've got an electric torch. They've got only one rifle and a revolver and damned little ammunition."

"I'd like to know where the Snow Hawk is," grumbled Koleff. "It was the MacLean guy that shot me."

"You'll have your chance to pay him back," Adler assured him.

They had waited then, enduring the chilling cold as they huddled in the darkness, until the outlaw chief at last gave the word. Then, with the torch flashing at brief intervals to pick up the trail, they had set out in single file through the bush.

No shots greeted them when they cautiously approached the tiny clearing. Silent as ghosts they had watched from behind the trees. Huddled beside the dying embers of a fire they distinguished one dark figure. It was Jean MacLean.

Peterson raised his gun. Blackjack Adler reached out and struck the weapon aside. Covering the girl with his own weapon—because he thought she might be in possession of the revolver—he strode out into the open.

Jean leaped to her feet. She did not cry out. Enduring almost intolerable suspense she had waited there beside the fire for that inevitable moment. Silently, she faced the four burly figures.

"So!" growled Adler, peering down at her. "Alone, eh? Where's the others?"

"Gone!" she replied dully.

"Don't lie to me!" said Adler, in a loud voice. "If any of them are waiting out there in the trees you'll die at the first shot they fire."

"They're gone!" she repeated.

"Where's the Snow Hawk—and the old man—and your brother?" demanded Adler fiercely.

"The Snow Hawk—and his father—went for help. They left this morning."

Adler uttered an explosive curse. "So that was the meaning of that trail in the snow!" he snarled. "Went for help, did they? And left you and your brother here! Well, your brother is dead."

In the distance they heard the crack of a rifle. The men looked at each other nervously. Then they heard another shot and another.

"Shooting!" gasped Brown.

For once in his life Blackjack Adler faced a situation that he could not fathom. The rifle shots were in the direction of the lake.

MacLean, whose absence still puzzled him, might be responsible for some of the shots, but not them all, for the distances varied.

Adler turned and glared at Jean. "You lied to me!" he snarled. "The Snow Hawk didn't go away."

"I have told you the truth!" she insisted firmly. "He went away this morning. Unless—unless—"

"What?"

"Unless he has come back with help."

Blackjack Adler laughed grimly. "We'll have a reception for him then, and for anyone with him." He made a sweeping gesture with his arm. "Men! Get into hiding. Peterson—go down the trail about ten yards. Drill the first man you see coming this way."

The Snow Hawk left the trail. There was just enough light from the snow, and from the aurora filtering through the branches above, to let him work his way into the woods beside the path without blundering into thickets or branches that would smash and crackle to betray his presence. The white parka flitted like a ghost among the trees.

Then he heard a voice: "Anyone coming yet?"

The voice came from the bush somewhere beyond the little clearing. It was answered by another.

"Thought I heard something a few minutes ago."

He stood rigid, trying to discover the man. A moment later he picked him out, a black shadow that melted almost indistinguishably into the dark mass of bush beside the trail.

The Snow Hawk crept toward the waiting figure. As silently as an animal of the woods, he advanced.

He was still beyond striking distance when one foot suddenly sank deep into the snow. A hidden clump of dry brush crashed noisily beneath his weight. In the cold, electric silence it was like a shattering explosion.

With a startled cry, the man swung around. The Snow Hawk caught the gleam of a rifle barrel as he plunged on. There was a spurt of flame, the crash of the shot. The wind of the bullet fanned his cheek. Gripping his own rifle by the barrel he swung viciously.

It crashed against Peterson before the man could pull the trigger for a second shot. He went down without a sound in a sprawled heap at the base of the tree and lay there without moving.

The Snow Hawk snatched up the man's rifle, wrenching it from the lax hands. He heard a shout.

"Did you get him?"

He cupped his gauntlet over his mouth to muffle his voice and called back: "Got him!"

There was an incredulous roar. Adler's voice, exultant, asked: "Not the Snow Hawk?"

"Come and see."

Three figures came into the clearing. One was Adler, with Jean struggling in his grasp. The other was Koleff. The Snow Hawk stepped out to the head of the trail and covered them with his rifle. They were out in the open before they saw the white-clad figure, before they realized the trap.

"Put up your hands!" he snapped.

And then, from the interior of the wrecked plane, came a warning shout: "Look out, son! There's another one of them."

Whang!

Beniah Brown, shrewdly waiting in hiding, on the off chance that this might be a trap, had opened fire. The Snow Hawk felt a searing pain across his side. Then the whole clearing was a confusion of noise and movement as Koleff and Adler leaped to their guns.

Adler, with a mighty sweep of his arm, sent Jean reeling directly into the line of fire. Koleff, with his free hand, brought up a revolver spitting lead. The Snow Hawk dodged in, fearful of hitting Jean if he shot. Out of the corner of his eye he saw Brown scrambling out from beneath the wreck. Adler's gun blazed just as the Snow Hawk raced across the clearing. Brown uttered a shriek, clawed at the air, and dropped dead from a bullet fired by Adler's gun.

Koleff backed away. A bullet from Koleff's revolver smashed into the Snow Hawk's left arm and knocked the rifle out of his grasp. Koleff came in at him with a roar of fury.

The Snow Hawk flung up his right arm and knocked the gun aside, butted Koleff and grappled with him. He could see Adler circling coolly, looking for an opening. Adler did not want to shoot his pilot by accident.

The Snow Hawk and Koleff went down in the snow, battling and struggling like wild cats. With his left arm useless and weakened by exhaustion and loss of blood from the wound in his side, the Snow Hawk hung on in a dim fog. Koleff was trying to twist the revolver around for a shot, but the Snow Hawk was hanging on like grim death to his wrist.

The pilot wrenched back his arm with a curse. The barrel of the gun raked the Snow Hawk's face. He grabbed the barrel and twisted violently. He wrenched it out of Koleff's hand and rolled. The pilot went sprawling, then leaped back at him in a fury. The gun barked. Koleff slumped on his face in the snow.

In the back of the Snow Hawk's mind was the knowledge that Adler was only waiting for the chance to drill a bullet through him without endangering Koleff's life. When the pilot tumbled over he wondered why the shot did not come. He twisted around, revolver in hand.

Adler was plunging in and struggling in the snow, with Jean clinging desperately to his arm. She had leaped forward just as the rifle was swinging down. Adler, cursing, flung her aside and stumbled forward, his finger groping for the trigger again.

The Snow Hawk could see the outlaw only as a huge figure in a mist. Half conscious, he could see the barrel of the rifle looming down upon him. He heard a shot. It seemed to come from a long distance away. Through the swimming fog he saw Adler falling. He felt a heavy weight suddenly collapse across his body. After that he knew nothing more.

Ten minutes later, when Ned Price and Tom Brooks broke into the clearing they found Matt Delaney and Jean MacLean binding up the Snow Hawk's wounds by the light of a blazing fire. Koleff and Peterson, both wounded, lay groaning near by. Beniah Brown lay where he had fallen beneath the wreck of the plane. And the firelight shone on the villainous dead face of Blackjack Adler, who had reached the end of his long trail of crime.

With Price and Brooks came Doug MacLean. Half frozen and almost overcome with exhaustion, he had found his way to the bush trail at last.

The Snow Hawk, regaining consciousness, saw Jean's face above him. "Am I going to be okay?"

"Of course," she told him.

"Sure he's going to get better," declared Matt Delaney. "Nothing wrong but a broken forearm and a creased rib. Snow hawks are hard to kill. You'll be well enough to pilot that plane out in the morning and send every Mounty in the country to round up the rest of that outfit in Killer's Valley."

"And after that," said Doug MacLean, warming himself beside the fire, "after that—the gold mine!"

Ned Price and Tom Brooks were speaking quietly to each other. The trapper came forward, awkwardly.

"Mr. Snow Hawk," he said, "I don't know what your real name is, but Tom and I owe you a kind of an apology. 'Course I know an apology isn't much, after chasing a fellow all over the country and trying to put a bullet through him, but—"

"The point is," said Delaney, "that you believe me now."

"Yes!" declared Ned Price and spat emphatically into the fire. "We believe you now. Any time you hit the trail again you can be sure of a welcome at my camp."

"He won't be hitting the trail again," said Matt Delaney. "The Snow Hawk is settling down from now on. Settling down to managing a gold mine."

Want more arctic adventure?

Read these **Checkmates**
by Leslie McFarlane

THE MYSTERY OF SPIDER LAKE

Constable Donovan is faced with a baffling double murder. Two bodies, clothed in light city suits, are found in the arctic wilderness—one manning a careening speedboat, the other dumped mysteriously from the sky into a snowdrift. The missing link, a fortune in corporate stocks and bonds, leads to a desperate chase by plane.

AGENT OF THE FALCON

What happens when Stephen Durant is innocently charged with murder? What happens when all the evidence points to him and the real murderers, a northern mining town gang, plot to kill him and the only man who can give him an alibi? Also included is another Snow Hawk adventure, and more . . .

Are you a hockey fan?

Read these **Checkmates**
by Leslie McFarlane

SQUEEZE PLAY

Tim Kiernan's brilliant defense brings his team into the final playoffs with everything in their favor. On the brink of success, blackmailers trick him into believing that he killed a man. His choice: to go to jail for murder or purposely bring defeat to his team.

THE DYNAMITE FLYNNS

Dan and Jerry Flynn, the toughest and tightest defensemen in the league, have only the final series ahead of them and are sure to win—but a malicious scheme involving an underworld figure, an accident in a stolen car, and jail stands in the way of success.

BREAKAWAY

A jealous cousin and an angry uncle join forces to squeeze Sniper out of major-league hockey by threatening legal action—until Sniper decides to fight fire with fire.